"Gabriela Damián Miravete is argu[ably one of the most import]ant writers of speculative fiction in Mexico, and her collection, *They Will Dream in the Garden*, showcases the breadth and depth of her work. Ranging from a bemused humanism reminiscent of Le Guin to disarming surrealism that reminds one of Murakami, these eleven stories are also deeply rooted in Mexico as place and culture and history. Damián Miravete masterfully wields semantics and syntax, trope and scheme, to draw us through unexpected layers in every piece, like delicate palimpsests that yield upon close observation startling phrases containing unforgettable truths. And balancing this technical skill is an emotional resonance, perhaps best felt in the harrowing and moving title story. *They Will Dream in the Garden* is a must-have for readers of literary and genre fiction alike, and let us hope that Gabriela captivates with such tales for many more years to come."

—David Bowles, award-winning author of *The Prince & the Coyote*

"Spun of nightmares and spiderwebs, this collection of stories by Gabriela Damián Miravete stretches from its roots in the Surrealist Movement to encompass the best and the worst of human imagination. Miravete brings us visions of worlds where animals and humans connect in mutual respect, women are valued for their abilities to empathize and collectively provide solutions, and the dead reach out to support the living in our daily worries. In addition, the collection includes the best psychotropic adventure story I have read. Every page of *They Will Dream in the Garden* is drenched in images of water. Every story gives us a chance to re-imagine ourselves in a world where feminism has won out against the evils of the drug trade, of patriarchy, and of machismo. If only. But we can dream."

—Kathleen Alcalá, author of *Spirits of the Ordinary*

"Luminous stories, haunted with memories as deep as the roots of the oldest ahuehuete, *They Will Dream in the Garden* is charged with a sense of justice that shows the world as it is, and as it could be."

—Christopher Brown, Philip K. Dick Award-nominated author of *Tropic of Kansas*

"In *They Will Dream in the Garden*, Gabriela Damián Miravete takes the speculative genres and makes them her own, so specific to Mexico but with that fairy tale quality of being anywhere or nowhere. This is a magnificent collection of short stories, with characters full of determination to invent and fashion with the tools they have, that never forgets that humans are the species that 'praises beauty while destroying it.'"

—Matthew David Goodwin, editor of *Latinx Rising* and co-editor of *Speculative Fiction for Dreamers*

They Will Dream in the Garden

Gabriela Damián Miravete

Translated by Adrian Demopulos

I would like to dedicate this book to my aunt Bertha and her sister Paulina, my grandmother, which is the same as saying that it is for all women who hold the soul of the world with dignity, love, and strength.

Rosarium Publishing
P.O. Box 544
Greenbelt, MD 20768-0544

www.rosariumpublishing.com

THEY WILL DREAM IN THE GARDEN

GABRIELA DAMIÁN MIRAVETE

Translated by Adrian Demopulos

TABLE OF CONTENTS

MUSIC AND PETALS

Tuesday

Every time I go down there I hear the music. I don't want to go. It scares me. The music is horrible. They yell my name. I know they're going to ask me to come down, and I don't want to. There's always something to get from Down There: casserole dishes, the mortar and pestle, the small grill, mineral spirits, or the special pot my mom uses to make chicken when someone comes over for dinner ... and it always has to be me who brings it up. Why? Sometimes mom sends my brother, but then he sends me; and I can't refuse, because if I do ...

Maybe what my brother does isn't worse than the music. But I don't like it.

It used to be fine going to the basement, making up stories about the paintings that aren't there anymore, or the trunk full of old fancy clothes from dead relatives, so stretched out they look like they were bought when they were already skeletons. Sometimes I would put them on and walk around wearing them among all the things Down There. I didn't have to be scared because I played with the lights on and did so many silly things. I remember one time I even ate a spiderweb to see what it tasted like (nothing, but it stuck terribly to the top of my mouth).

Until I started to hear the music.

How would I describe it? *Da da da ... dada dum dadadum ...*

There's a reason why some very smart people invented a method to write down how music sounds because when I put it like that, I don't think you can understand it. There are notebooks Down There with the piano lessons that my brother abandoned years ago, but all the same, I don't want to go.

I want to describe how it sounds. Sometimes I feel like, if someone else could hear it, they'd say, "You poor thing, what you have to put up with!"

And then I wouldn't feel so alone.

Monday

New neighbors moved in today. My mom says that house, which is next to ours, used to be our relatives' cigar factory. There they would de-stem the leaves and leave them out to dry, which always smelled amazing, like San Andres Negro[1] without the burning. And at one point their basement and ours were connected. My jaw dropped imagining how enormous Down There would be if they were put together. Mom stroked my hair.

I dared to ask, "Do you hear music sometimes?"

"What did you say?" she responded with a little laugh that made everything clear. If she heard it, she would have said, "Yes, and I don't want you to hear it, too."

She has no idea, poor mom. It's better that way.

***

---

1   Made only with black tobacco planted in the town of San Andrés Tuxtla, Veracruz.

Friday

The new neighbors are young. The wife is very pretty, with dark hair and delicate features. The skin on her! Just like polished wood. If you get close, she smells delicious, like a new serving spoon. I didn't see the husband, but another neighbor said he looks like the Spanish priests in paintings. Maybe I'll meet him this afternoon.

My brother has been very quiet, but it looks like the new neighbor has him worked up. We'll see if he stops bothering me. I don't want to hear the music. Everything seems so normal right now ...

The first time I heard it I was walking down the stairs. I had been asked to bring up a wool blanket because the wind was blowing hard and it gets chilly on nights like that. The melody was hollow, muffled, like it was behind a wall. I thought maybe someone was playing an instrument in the house next door, practicing the same melody over and over, a very short one, insistently. But obviously, the house was empty. There's nothing else to say, just the air blowing inside of a metal tube to repeat that phrase. What could it be saying?

When I hear it I feel the same sadness as when we visited the lighthouse on the port. The siren sounded to me like a wailing moan, but mom said the lighthouse saves boats that get lost at sea in the night. It seemed to me like the lighthouse was screaming, "Turn back now because the real danger is here, here there is nothing." That's what the music sounds like.

It's hard to explain. Maybe the day I can do that is the day I'll stop hearing it.

Saturday

My brother is a hypocrite. When mom is around, the son of a bitch is a saint. I don't tell on him because it would be a huge disappointment for her, and with how much she works and how lonely she is ...

Yesterday the idiot was lurking around between the backs of the two houses, taking advantage of the grass overgrown from the rain to hide. I saw him staring at the neighbor, who wasn't doing anything special, just rearranging junk in the kitchen and looking everywhere for a package that she then opened desperately. Then the husband caught him. Luckily, my brother was only watching, but the man was really mad anyway.

"What do you want?" he said harshly.

"Nothing, I heard an animal wandering around back here," said his voice, which I loved to hear filled with so much fear.

The man, to my surprise, must have sensed me because he turned to look at me in my clumsy hiding place behind the curtains. My brother turned, too, and just by seeing his face, I knew what would happen to me later.

The man called for his wife. Her name on his lips sounded strange, severe. My brother said goodnight and entered the house quickly between stalks and mosquitos.

"Let's go downstairs," he said.

"No," I answered in a thin whisper of a voice as he pulled my hair and dragged me to the stairs behind the door. I heard the music again when my brother turned off the light Down There; and he, like the rest of the clutter, turned to shadow.

Sometimes I don't know what's worse, the music or my brother's muffled voice.

In the back of my head, the melody echoes, accompanied by a deep, dry groan, the combination submerging me in a dense stupor. I feel so heavy that I sink. I feel like I'm paralyzed, but the strangest part is that it's not my body that can't move, it's *me.* Nevertheless, there I am. I see everything happening in front of me while the notes repeat, while my legs prickle with the sensation that the falling will never end and the thing I feel that is me and not my body submerges in a black well of thick water, the music taking hold of my hands, my flesh ...

My brother puts his eternal idiot face back on to go up the stairs. And it's then that I return from that darkness, that death.

It wasn't like this before. The first times were very short.

But now he's more resistant each time. More dissatisfied.

Monday

Today I went out for a walk by the river and found the neighbor wandering barefoot on the shore. Come here, she said. Will you help me? I stood in front of her, and she held onto my arm. She lifted one of her tiny, tiny feet, and with the opposite hand she removed the thorn that had gotten stuck there. She thanked me with the flirtatiousness that I lack. She wrapped herself in her sweater, necessary because of the strange fog falling in the area recently. She rummaged through her pockets and took out a cigarette that she lit like elegant ladies do. She talked about a lot of things, but I didn't pay much attention until the wind gave me a shiver and she touched my arm. Are you cold? I have hot chocolate at the house, come on over. And I went.

Her house was just like mine, even though the factory smell was still there. The neighbor served the hot chocolate in very pretty blue mugs, her fingers holding her tight curls far away from her face. It hurt me a little. I sensed that she was lonely, more than anything, because she started chatting with me like I was a girlfriend her age. She even asked me if I had a boyfriend (I went red, obviously).

"You're very cute. If I did your hair like this and like this" (she said while she lifted my hair in a little crown,

15

twisted it at the ends, fastened it with pins) "we'd have to chase your suitors away." Suddenly, her face turned sad, she looked at me, and with a sigh, said, "But you still have a girl's curiosity."

If only she knew. I didn't know if someone could get drunk on hot chocolate, but my face felt boiling hot and my voice felt bold, so I hit her with the question.

"Do you like your basement?"

She laughed, and answered, "Do you like yours? Come on," she said, and I followed her for the third time.

We opened the door that led to the other Down There, and a colorless face jumped out at us, pale like the paraffin of candles, eyes miles away, glassy. Her husband.

"We're coming down," she warned.

The man didn't answer. He just looked at her, captivated and crippled like a wax doll that had fallen, disoriented, from its pedestal. Then he walked right past us.

The basement, compared to ours, has fewer objects displayed. There are stacks and stacks of boxes, some old furniture, others that belonged to the cigar factory. Better lit, for sure.

"I heard that our basements are connected," I spoke, still drunk on chocolate.

"Yes. That's where the passage was." She gestured toward the wall with a languid hand. "It's sealed up now."

I wasn't expecting that response. I got closer. Between boxes and wooden crates I saw in the wall the outline of a silhouette, that of a door, maybe. It looked like an irregular, shiny scar that spoke of a wound suffered by both houses. Leaning on the same wall was an elegant black case. The case of some musical instrument.

"It was my father's," she said, as if she had read my mind. "El Negro," she said, kicking the words out of her mouth in bitter mockery.

That's how it started, that was it. I felt uncomfortable, but again, I thought of her loneliness. Talking about her family, now that she was married and far away from them, was only logical.

"They kept him here in the corner. Tied up. You know how people were with their slaves."

She opened the case with her long brown fingers. Inside, there was a kind of long flute with many keys and little tubes coming out of the sides.

"It's called a bassoon. God knows how it works," she said, somewhere between disdainful and smiling.

She closed the case. She grabbed the rag stuck in her apron to clean the tops of the boxes covered in dust.

"Your family had my father since he was a kid. He was their worker. You must know what they say: that it was my father who gave your uncle, the crazy one, his sickness. But that's not true. Everyone knows it was the other way around ... but they had to blame the Black man ..."

She looked at me, anguished. "I don't think I should be talking to you about this ..." and the tawny color of her face turned brick red.

"I know the story, my mom tells it every now and then," I said. Lie. My mom hates talking about that. She hates to remember that my brother is like my father's side of the family, hates remembering that they, so fair and so pure, preferred to marry among themselves, that she had been one of the beans in the rice of their French lineage. They hated us so much for staining their bloodline that they only begrudgingly let us live in our house when my dad died.

"Then you know why I'm here," she said. I imagine my dumb face was evident because she let out a long sigh, sat on a wooden crate and taking out the small package that she was looking for the other day, continued the story.

"My father took this to stay strong and clearheaded," she said while showing me the handful of colorful petals contained in the package.

"What is it?" I asked.

"Another kind of tobacco," she answered with a strange shine in her eyes, like she was holding back laughter. It smelled like a mix of vanilla and that secret smell men have that I've only known in my brother. "My father worked with your uncle. He liked something about him. He dragged him everywhere," she started to say, grabbing a little fistful of petals, some dry, others soft. "He was his right hand until my father fell in love with my mother and I was born. But you know what your uncle was like, or didn't they tell you?"

She didn't give me time to respond, and I don't think she expected me to say anything. She squinted her eyes as if to focus on the image of that omnipresent man in my house, on the objects Down There, on the dusty photographs that my mother never wants to even touch.

"He was very ignorant, aggressive. Whatever he wanted, he got it. But he was made weak by desire." Now the neighbor put the petals on her tongue. "He had his eyes on my mom. White as he was—just like your brother—he thought there was nobody who could resist him, but there was no way to get my mom by playing fair ... so he poisoned my father with these," she said, shaking the petals, which sounded alive, like pebbles swept up in the rain. "He went crazy. He howled. I remember."

Outside, the cicadas and geckos were the only sound of twilight. I felt my skin sticky and damp in this place where the world above filtered in: the steam of the hot chocolate, the perfume of the man of the house, the aftertaste of the lime that whitened the walls, the sweet scent of those petals. Where, what trees or branches did they bloom on?

The woman chewed two or three like they were tobacco. Her eyes widened, looking blacker, shinier. She looked at me strangely, but it didn't scare me. I wanted to know.

"Your uncle was insane from birth. My father, insane by design." With that last phrase she started laughing roughly, her curls getting more and more tangled. "He worked by day, and when it got dark, he shut himself in here, in the basement. They thought we would take him away if he stayed with us, in our miserable little house. We couldn't even decide to take our sadness somewhere else.

"My mother dressed in her Sunday best every time we came to the basement, as if talcum powder or lipstick would put him back in his right mind. But it wasn't his wife, wasn't his daughter: it was music that brought back a little of his peace. Your uncle had given him his bassoon because he never learned how to play well. He was a slacker, he was lazy. He was a pig. He preferred to entertain himself with other things, spawning children with his sisters or his sisters-in-law, even though they were married. My father learned to play the bassoon while he walked around his enclosure, the kingdom of his basement. He was a real Yanga[2], my father. He played beautifully ..."

The neighbor half-shut her eyes, suddenly illuminated. Everything seemed brilliant, splendid to me in that moment. I don't know if she realized.

"As if he were talking to us through music. The beautiful things he couldn't say, he blew them into the notes, inflating them like balloons so we could understand them, to caress us with the arms of the melody.

"Want more?"

She offered me the package, its tenuous petals of beautiful colors. Then I understood that she had put them in my hot chocolate. I laughed more at the realization. I shook my head and got carried away in the soft sensation. The neighbor continued, her dark eyelashes shadowing her cheeks.

"My mom would bring me to visit, also dressed up, ribbons in my hair. What a great and dark man, my father.

2   Yanga: location some 150 kilometers from the port of Veracruz, inhabited by slaves brought from Africa that rose against Spanish colonialism on January 6th, 1609, making it the first free town of the Americas. It is named in honor of Gaspar Nyanga, leader of the rebellion, who is often called a *prince* or *warrior*.

His eyes shone through the thickness of the basement, very white, very open. He would take me in his arms and kiss me with such care, as if I would break. He adored my mother. He would touch her cheeks, look at her for a long time. And then he would start to cry. He would pick up the bassoon and play those pretty songs that he wrote himself. Until your uncle ... well. After that he only played the same melody, over and over again, an incomplete, off-key, horrible song."

The neighbor lost her gaze in the corner of the basement like she was watching an atrocity. Then I felt an emptiness in my stomach because the music, my music, came out of her mouth: *Da da da ... dada dum dadadum ...* Then she looked at me. Her eyes looked desperate. She was quiet for a moment. Then her delicate face transformed.

"Your uncle defiled her, right here. My father tied up there, staring. I was sleeping. I knew my mother was brave, that she would do something after an outrage like that. That's why he killed her." She looked at the petals in bewilderment, took a couple. Her eyes changed again, deep and compassionate like an animal's. "Oh, you pretty thing, the world is such shit," she said, her voice breaking.

Tuesday

"I don't like you snooping around with the neighbor. Her husband is a snob," mom said to me today.

"You know we're almost like family?" I answered sarcastically. I had never talked to her like that. I thought she would be mad, but instead she looked surprised.

"I figured that," she responded. Which confirms that my mother knows everything. Does she also know about my brother, about me ...?

In any case, we're so miserable that my misfortune has no room to inherit a house that pays for the sins of its demented son.

Wednesday

I've asked the other neighbors what they know about my uncle's death. "He died by his own hand," they said. They also said that he was treated for Espanto, but it had no effect. Others thought he was cursed; others, that he died overcome with rage. What they all said is that the coffin was empty, who knows why. Nobody thought it was strange because the family was just like that: strange, detached. Indifferent. That's the way crazy people are.

I didn't even need to ask about "El Negro." As soon as they started whispering about my new friend, the theories rolled off their long tongues: that he killed a child, he fled by night on a cloud-colored horse, his enormous blood-covered hands staining its mane.

The other women on our street treated the neighbor well when they met her face to face, but behind her back they talked about her insolence, about how revealing her skirt was, how she didn't wear a bra. How her husband must be out of his mind to not realize what he has in the house.

She greets me normally, pretending she never told me anything. I haven't heard the music again. My brother is off entertained somewhere else, and I, happy, help my mom wash the mountain of clothes she has to do, imagining that she and I are alone and that we're all each other needs in this world.

Thursday

I saw what happened from behind the curtains.

My brother was talking to the neighbor. He brought some records, put them on. She entertained him for a little bit, but then she was very uncomfortable. She didn't sit down with him at all. She isn't the woman the others say she is. I don't think any woman is what the neighbors describe, what they love to insult. Then my brother got very close to her. She opened the back door to make him leave. He started to protest with words and rude gestures. The neighbor pouted, made the same face that children make when they're about to cry, but she didn't return his stupid remarks. I wanted to leave, go to where mom was, surely in one of the houses where she went to iron. But when I opened the door, in that strange fog, hot as it was, he got out in front of me. "Let's go," he said, his voice filled with that smell.

As we went down the stairs, my brother shouted terrible things about how women only live to tease, to be the bane of men's lives, that we enjoyed being stupid. He tugged my hair, bit me, and squeezed my flesh, my poor flesh that started to become paralyzed, hearing the music. We stumbled over the piano bench, the sheet music scattering on the floor like a deck of cards. Would the horrible melody that got closer and closer be written there? The shapeless mass of sweat, blond hair, and tongue that was my brother on top of me, and the music!

A hopeless din choked me endlessly. Then the music synchronized its rhythm with that of my heart, obscuring everything. The light breath that was *me* went numb in sleep. My still body suddenly opened its eyes, other eyes. My hands, other hands, raised thickly against the white neck of that man, and squeezed and squeezed ...

My brother hit my girl face, but my face, another face, slammed against his, and I bit him and devoured his cheeks in little pieces that I realized were sweet, the sweetness of pork and the warmth of blood in my mouth, another mouth, a big mouth, with extremely white teeth. And then my whole body, another body, tall and furious, got my brother to the ground with kicks and bites; I stripped his skin away by hitting him with stones, beat and dismembered his limbs with blows.

My body, this other body made of music, of pure melody, knocked down, in a rage, the wall that divided the two basements, and I threw the teeth and the arms and the hair of almost pure lineage in there, along with other vile bones, already old and eaten. Then my splendid body, my other fibrous, sonorous body, looked for something to close the hole in the wall.

I guess this time the music was hard to ignore. My mom had already come down to the basement, Down There, with me. She waited for me at the foot of the stairs, carrying a shovel and a sack of plaster.

THE END OF THE PARTY

The day will come when, after harnessing the ether, the winds, the tides, gravitation, we shall harness for God the energies of love. And, on that day, for the second time in the history of the world, man will have discovered fire.

—Pierre Teilhard de Chardin

At nine in the morning, after tripping on the bowl of water Fénix dragged to the middle of the kitchen as a form of protest, Verónica put out enough cat food, took out the two trash bags, and yelled, "Be right back, Fénix!" from the front door. The animal, a skinny hairless cat, half-opened his yellow eyes. Trotting toward her, he grumbled his response in a series of growls and vague noises.

"No," she said, "I won't be right back. But I will be back, just like every other time you've seen me leave, silly cat."

In response, Fénix meowed a little cry of annoyance mixed with a yawn and turned away. His serpentine tail disappeared behind the corner of the hallway.

It was cold. She could feel her fingers frozen solid on the steering wheel. The morning, however, was sunny and bright, the whiteness of the clouds outlined by the light depths of blue. She thought about how Fénix would miss out on these fabulous sights because their new neighbor was a bitter guy who couldn't stand to see him prowling on the balcony. And, well, he was right: the stupid cat had left a few souvenirs in his flower box.

The only thing Fénix hated were birds: they brought out the worst of his instincts. One afternoon of feline glory he managed to hunt down a sparrow. Unfortunately, he decided to do it there in an area more attractive than his house. But what would he know about neighborly cohabitation? Animals don't understand property, that this is mine and not in any way yours. Fénix thought he owned the ground he walked on and didn't require any contract to confirm it, even less after seven years of coming and going on a whim. Sure, he had gotten lazy and sometimes preferred to sleep all day instead of walking on the parapet to the inhospitable terrain of the next-door balcony. He only remembered to do it every once in a while, then he returned renewed and content, tail held high. But now he had lost this chance.

It made Verónica sad to think that, locked up in the house by himself all day, the poor thing wouldn't have much of a social or family life (castrated at the age of six months, as he was). He must be fatally bored seeing only her face every day. Maybe she should adopt another cat so that he could live a little more of his life of nights and claws, scents and silence. Unlike Fénix, Verónica had an affectionate family, helicopter-like, who wouldn't leave her alone, rain or shine, like right now, when her telephone rang.

"Did you leave already? Why didn't you answer your house phone?"

"Like you said, I already left."

"Have you heard the news?"

"No. But hey, I wanted to tell you that I don't know if I'll make it."

"Will you be out late? We were thinking of waiting for you, even if you don't get here until the end. That's the best part of the party ..."

"I don't know if I can. I'll let you know, Dad."

There was an unorganized caravan of cars in front of Verónica. Some people were sitting in their windows, an everyday thing in the city, but it was the attitude of the people that lent the atmosphere its feeling of doom. Hardly anybody was honking their horns. Rather, they were interrogating one another, talking on the phone, passing through doors and windows to see what happened.

"Nobody's moving. Something happened here. Do you know what's going on?"

"You haven't even turned on the radio?"

"I haven't had one for a while. It overwhelms me."

A sigh of impatience came from the receiver. "There's a kind of network failure going on everywhere. A satellite or God knows what fucked up the telecommunications. We've heard about a video that's going around, but we haven't seen it. I even thought I wouldn't be able to reach you."

The wandering drivers continued their hunt for any news about the traffic. They also talked on their cellphones or tapped out text messages with speedy fingers.

"Well, I'll let you know soon. But don't wait for me."

"And how will you let me know if ...?"

"I'll be there, I'm telling you. But it'll be at the end."

"I hope you come. Everyone will be here."

After a while the most timid drivers, like Verónica, started leaving their cars. They made their way through the cars to the small crowd that had met farther down around a man who was moving desperately, back and forth, holding a tablet that he showed to one person, then another, without anyone really being able to see the video that was playing, which only lasted a few seconds. Some laughed nervously, others rubbed the back of their necks, a couple tried to talk to him, to get a word out, the usual helpers wanted to comfort him, touched him, and talked to him like a child. Anyone who tried to touch the screen got a start because the guy really wanted to show it, but not give it to anyone else. Several people dove into their phones, trying to find the video. Some, who had seen a part of it, commented among themselves.

"It has to be fake."

Verónica stayed standing, disconcerted and detached from the racket, feeling compassion for the man, his immeasurable anguish. As if letting her know that, somehow, he heard her, he approached her, holding the tablet without looking away from her, waiting for her reaction.

Inside of a room, the lamp, the stool, the pencils lift from their surfaces and spin slowly. The person holding the camera leans over the balcony. Everything looks the same, a subtle elevation: the branches and leaves on the trees, the cables. The birds look surprised and quiet in suspended flight. Suddenly, a piece of the horizon disappears. This is the part most difficult to explain to the eye that sees it: in place of this piece of reality, of landscape, of sky, trees, grass, there's nothing, nothing remains. This blind spot, irreparable, nonexistent, captivates the cameraman: he zooms in, his breathing picks up speed.

The thing, the nothing, extends like a ravenous spiral that spins almost imperceptibly, consuming more pieces of the horizon like water progressively creeping, slowly and quickly, harmless and definitive at the same time. Everything seems flooded by a disagreeable white noise. You can hear the puff of breath, the astonished breathing of the person recording this moment. In it, in the loss of the image, the fleeing that stops the recording, you sense the drive to share this discovery, this kind of ultimate revelation.

Verónica looked at the screen, waiting for something else to happen. The man searched for her gaze desperately. When he found it, he sustained it, as if a network of fear and compassion stretched between them. But they couldn't find anything to say. They shared in silence the certainty that this would reach them sooner or later. It was, more than the sharing of a fact, the feeling that it would take over everything: that proximity to this void would lead, little by little, to chairs no longer being chairs, apples losing their colorful juicy fruit qualities; the people would be replaced by that darkness, that blindness, that nothing. She herself, having seen it, already felt incomplete. There was something of hers that had ceased to be, but she didn't know how to say what it was. The commotion of people around got louder. They called her, they asked her what she thought it *was*. Verónica let those who had seen the video from the side, next to her, respond.

She dialed her father's number. The call didn't go through. After several tries, she reached them. Would they know? Had they already lost something, like her?

They couldn't hear her on the other end, but she shouted into the phone, "I'm on my way, but I don't know when I'll be there. I have to get Fénix."

Getting off the main route wasn't easy. Verónica waited a bit until the road was cleared to maneuver through. With some effort she got the car over the median to escape through one of the side roads. The tires emitted that burnt smell that repels anyone who detects it in catastrophes.

The difference from the highway was notable, but the streets were full of cars. The sky and its transparency mocked the concert of voices and horns, contrasted with the tangled landscape of cars climbing anywhere to go faster, the parents of children crowding in the doorways of schools, their children carrying their backpacks, ready to leave without knowing why. Verónica turned on a street going south, another going east. Some were still deserted, like they were waiting; and others were interminable intersections. That's how she moved, little by little, while the hours seemed to ignore the time that people inhabited.

After the frequent earthquakes the city had suffered a few years back, Verónica had designed a strategy to keep Fénix safe. It embarrassed her a little to tell her family, who remained in respectful silence around everything concerning the cat, despite the fact that it seemed exaggerated to worry about him so much, to love an animal so much (who, on top of that, was ugly). She knew what they thought, but she didn't care much. She had gone over the plan several times. She had a tube—similar to a tube of toothpaste—of super-concentrated nutrients, a sweet translucent paste that the vet had given her to stimulate his appetite when he was sick and wouldn't eat anything. "Use it on his nose or a paw. He won't be able to stand the feeling of being dirty and will have to lick it off."

If something terrible were to happen, Verónica would take the cage (the *taxi*, the employees at the store had called it when she bought it) and put Fénix in without accepting any protests. She wasn't sure how she would achieve this last part if the miserable thing hid behind the chairs every time he heard the inoffensive click of the latch opening. The cage would have, on the sides, little baskets filled with enough food and water for some time. She wondered how the hell it hadn't occurred to her to prepare a little food and water for herself as well. It wouldn't hurt, considering she was the one who had to feed Fénix, and at least for this task, she needed to ensure her own survival. But did it matter to think about such strategies now? Maybe not. In every street the same shape repeated: people looking to communicate.

Home wasn't that much farther, but at noon, with the sun in the middle of the sky, isolated, uproarious, searching screams sounded. At the same time a cold wind blew, howling between the stuck cars. The panic caused a line of cars to launch in the opposite direction to escape the growing crowd and get into the guarded streets of the area. Verónica joined them and could see that the doors of the houses were open, that windows were shattered here and there, that many dogs, disoriented, were headed for the parks. There were empty streets and others dotted with groups of people. There were also heads, remaining crouched, that peeked out at the passing cars.

Hours later, when Verónica turned the corner onto her street, she found the gates open and the buildings apparently empty. There was no light. She parked the car quickly and climbed the two stories in a blink. On the landing was a blanket piled up along with other objects. She opened the door to her house, which was still dark and cold. She called Fénix over and over. Not a trace of the damn animal, that's typical, she thought. She looked for him under the seats, the refrigerator, above the cupboards, in her wardrobe.

There he was. He had climbed behind the coats until one fell to rest on top of him in the very back. He had his ears back, and his eyes were black, tail bristled like that of a squirrel. Verónica couldn't hold back a chuckle. She remembered when the girls from the animal shelter brought Fénix home, he had the exact same expression as now. Since she first saw this animal with thin, messed-up fur the color of ash, who had lived an entire month without his mother inside of a dumpster, she felt a deep sympathy for him. The reddish veins that reached over his face and paws looked to Verónica like the glimmers of a flame, a fire that persists in the rain.

She took him from the closet and put him on the floor. He gave a few meows of distress, melodramatic and grave, very different from the sharp, spoiled voice that demanded his breakfast. The cat's legs buckled like a newborn goat, and Verónica laughed more at the tragic spirit of Fénix. She spoke to him gently, petted his head. The cat half-closed his eyes and got into the cage without putting up too much resistance.

Verónica, feeling in higher spirits, wanted to gather a few things to bring to her family (candles, matches, canned foods), hoping at the same time that she didn't need them, that the situation were different over there, but she had barely managed to put some of her things in with Fénix before she heard louder, more intense voices. She stopped and only moved again after a moment when she no longer heard anything and it seemed opportune to leave.

What else should she take? She took a glance at the living room. Now she noticed it: there were so many things in her house. So many of them were precious to her. They left quickly and unstealthily. A group of people blocked her path and jumped on the car. Though she was scared, she didn't stop. She almost didn't at all until she reached the inspection point on the road.

It had already started to get dark when the interminable line to the exit moved forward, stopping and starting. She started to panic: they were discriminating with criteria that surely she didn't meet, she who never carried her complete papers, who had never been eligible for a loan. People pulled over until it was impossible to ignore the officials that threatened them with their guns if they didn't stop. There were more of that group than there were people who were allowed to leave, free, on the highway. Fénix let out an opera-style meow every now and then, when the cold, cyclical blizzard approached. But now he was very serious, standing straight up in his cage.

"Residents only," the officer spat when her turn came.

"Yes, I'm a resident."

"You have to prove it."

She rummaged nervously through the glove box and found, mercifully, a card she used to enter the housing complex where her parents lived. It had the correct address and her license plates in big numbers and letters.

The man examined it without much interest and asked for her identification. Fénix watched his every movement from the cage with a very formal cat expression. The man looked at him for a second, too. He raised his pen and pointed out an improvised road that ran parallel to the freeway. Verónica couldn't believe it.

"That way. Don't turn your lights off at any point."

The road was full of ruts and boulders that didn't let her move quickly. A solitary line of cars left their red trails in front of Verónica and Fénix, who had become hysterical with the turbulence of the car. He meowed bump after bump, and though Verónica tried to calm him down, the cat raised his voice even more. Fed up, she opened the cage and let him out. Fénix sat in the passenger's seat, leaned out of the window a few times, then lay down. Curled up in a little ball, he slept without another sound.

After a few hours, the road diverged from the freeway. The cars that preceded her had disappeared a while ago, incorporating themselves onto the freeway, onto other detours, or into the woods. She couldn't tell where they were. Night had fallen, and only a glow, maybe from the moon, lit the way. She resolved to stop for a moment and try to locate herself using the guide in the trunk. She looked through the things she had thrown back there years ago. She was surprised to find a pair of shoes that she never took to get the heels replaced and let out a laugh when she recognized, between an umbrella and a bag filled with spare parts, a picture frame with the photo of her grandmother she thought was lost. She picked it up along with the guide. When she was about to get back into the car, she saw the puny figure of Fénix, his eyes crusty from sleep, squinting in the glare of the headlights.

"Fénix!"

The cat kept still until Verónica tried to grab him. Then he opened his eyes wide and leapt into the trees. She ran after him until she realized that she would never find him without light. She got the car as close to the forest as possible, turning on the high beams, cursing the entire time.

"Stupid cat. Stupid cat ..."

She walked between the trunks and grass that the rays of light defined against the black horizon. She shouted for Fénix several times and then made those little noises that people use to attract cats (mostly without success) so as to not attract the attention of anyone passing by. Little by little, the milky light of the car was losing its range. Verónica, in the dark, shrunk into the heart of a forest vaster than she had imagined.

What if she didn't find Fénix ever? Would it be better for him?

The light of the car was only an echo of a gleam. She grasped the cage with her cold fingers. She would make him come back with the smell of the food and trap him there the entire trip until she got home, which would serve him right, she thought. She distinguished the thin trunks of the trees and the smell of night mixed with a perfume of firewood. The silence reigning there seemed indifferent to what was happening. Verónica felt like a witness to a serene conversation between the elements of this place, only interrupted by her own breathing, visible in the air like a silky vapor ascending to the highest fronds. The illuminated path became fragmented in tiny echoes of light until she could no longer see anything. She called Fénix again and again, paralyzed by the darkness and the growing fear of having lost him. She felt the back pocket of her pants and let out a sigh of relief when she felt her phone, which she immediately used as a flashlight. It occurred to her to shine the light on the high parts of the trees in case the cat had taken to climbing. She was able to see several tails and pairs of eyes that hid themselves speedily from the blue light she aimed at them, but none of them belonged to Fénix. She felt the violent urge to cry.

The forest was getting steeper. After walking uphill for a while, Verónica discerned a pronounced slope crowned by an orange halo. She got closer and saw, in the middle of a clearing, a house, well-lit despite its ruinous appearance, flanked by what she guessed were a corral and a pigsty.

Only when she was already very close did she see the horde of dogs of all colors and sizes rushing toward her, some wagging their tails amiably, others barking with distrust. A woman emerged from the door of the house. Against the light only her hair, very short, and her silhouette, small but strong, sturdy, were visible.

"Who is it?!" she demanded in a firm, slightly shrill voice.

Verónica didn't know how to answer. In this moment, she was nobody. Not somebody, at least, whose circumstances were easy to explain. Greeting her was the only thing she could think to do. She walked faster, trying to ignore the affectionate leaps or startled grumbles of the dogs. She wanted to explain herself face to face instead of shouting.

The woman was wearing a T-shirt and a skirt, and her thick, short legs were bare. Only her feet were covered with something that looked warm: some shoes made of velvety black cloth with a colorful flower embroidered on the upper.

"Balón! Negra! Satanás! Come here!"

The dogs switched gears instantly. They folded their ears back, lowered the unstoppable pendulums of their tails, and returned to her with resigned devotion.

"I'm sorry for the fuss. I got lost looking for my cat. He jumped out of the car, and I lost him ..." Verónica was embarrassed to speak in a voice so full of self-pity, tears falling against her will. But the woman, older than her, had understanding eyes that softened her wrinkled and severe face.

The wind picked up in violent swells. The turkeys got worked up and provoked bleating from the sheep. The woman looked at the sky for a moment and went inside.

"Come on in."

The kitchen took up almost all of the house. Pots and ladles hung from the walls, two or three meals bubbled on the stove. A cat dozed on the table, its tail coming and going over a stack of embroidered napkins. The woman spat some reprimand along with a heavy smack, and the cat went flying, getting lost behind a pink curtain patterned with blue flowers.

"It doesn't work," said the woman, repeatedly pushing the buttons of an alarm clock. "The radio. My son went to get his. Do you have a radio?"

Verónica said no, as if admitting to the old woman that she was going to be useless, even though she obviously would be a burden. She didn't know where she was, she was hungry and in a hurry to get out. The woman shrugged her shoulders.

"The radio said there was a global crisis, but it wouldn't get to Mexico. Earthquakes and hurricanes all over. God protect us, I said to my son. But he said that the best thing is to stay home because the weather is what's going to be affected. That's what my son said, but I know it's a lie. I heard when they said it would get dark, that there was a hole through the sky, and that the big buildings were lifting off the ground out there in China or Australia. I see the sky acting strangely. And the lambs have been scared for days seeing the wind come like it is right now. The animals know better. My dogs go and hide under my skirts ... but you saw, these goddamned cats don't care ..."

The woman let out a refreshing laugh made of water. Verónica noted that every wrinkle in her face had been caused just by her laughter. They traced on her face the kind map of her humor. She rose and began serving the contents of the pots on a plate and in a cup.

"You lost your cat, you said?"

Verónica felt a hole in her stomach. The moment that the woman's laugh had created collapsed with no remedy. She explained that they came from the city and that the blockades made them take the road through the forest, but when she wanted to find her way with the guide, the cat had run off and she couldn't catch him.

"You're not too far. You'd have to take the exit up ahead, and it's not too long after that," she encouraged.

Verónica ate slowly. She longed for food, but the absence of Fénix chased away her appetite on every other bite. But knowing that it wouldn't be much longer before she could see her family lightened her mood a bit.

The thundering of fireworks came from outside. But, judging by the woman's face, it might have been the echo of a gunshot. The dogs barked vehemently and trotted solemnly to the edge of the clearing to investigate the situation.

The woman stood up. Walking like a duck, she went through the curtain and returned, putting on a sweater of woven wool with patterns that Verónica thought were beautiful. She noted that the woman was very strong, but in certain movements it was clear that she was much older than she seemed, with that hair so black and her energetic arms. She examined the sky. The lambs bleated more calmly. To Verónica, it felt like they were calling to the woman like they had seen her leave. Her brow was furrowed, and she pet the dogs distractedly. A couple of kittens also came out to see her and rubbed against her legs. The old woman emerged from her meditation and took them by the neck. Smiling, she entered the house, and said with a cheerful smile, "My cat will bring him to you. You'll see. Come on, look."

Verónica followed her to the room hidden by the curtain. On the corner of a large, soft bed covered in cushions embroidered with colorful thread lay an enormous cat, very well-groomed, surrounded by kittens. The woman spoke to her in a mellifluous, soft tone until she opened her eyes. She looked Verónica up and down with her blue Siamese eyes and sniffed her while she listened to the old woman's explanation, moving her ears toward her voice like two triangular antennae.

"What's his name?"

"Fénix."

"That's quite a name, honey." She pet the cat's back with tough tenderness while she spoke. "Go get Fénix, Chula, okay? Bring him back to his friend, who loves him like I love you."

The cat brought her little snout close to the old woman's face and shut her eyes. The dogs started barking again. Chula opened her eyes wide, leapt gracefully from the bed to the floor, and ran to the door.

"That must be my son because the dogs got so happy."

They followed her. The turkeys made such a commotion that they unsettled the pigs in turn. The dogs alternated their gazes between the outside and the two women in frank confusion. Chula passed through them and meowed capriciously at a figure moving low to the ground. A pair of scared, fluorescent eyes stared at her from the shadows.

It was Fénix.

The fiercest dogs continued barking, but the cat summoned his courage and crossed the barrier when he heard Verónica's affectionate voice. With his tail extremely fluffed he jumped to the table to let her pet him and immediately searched for the door of his taxi with his snout.

The old woman laughed and laughed and, presuming the episode was finished, hurried back to her chores. She collected the dishes from the table, went out to converse with the pigs, and filled two buckets with water from the basin.

Suddenly, Verónica felt she wanted to stay in this place that seemed untouched by the horrors of the world. But she still felt something was missing, some absence that seemed to be right under her nose. Fénix looked at her from the cushy interior of the cage. She scratched behind his ears, fastened the bolt, and went to help the woman, even though she seemed to have no trouble carrying one pail after another on her own. Verónica shredded pieces of tortilla for the pigs and accompanied the woman in her rounds through the corral. The hens napped, fluffy and defenseless, in the darkness.

"I have my chickens, my turkeys, my water ... Aren't we rich, Balón?" she said to the fat, short-legged dog who followed her everywhere. "Once my son gets here, I'll have everything," she said with a cheerful gravity that she maintained when addressing Verónica. "You have to go looking for your parents. They must be worried sick."

Verónica agreed, immersed in the woman's liquid gaze, which looked back at her. Mother. Father. Sister. Son. That was what they were saying when they looked at each other. It wasn't one of those distracted gestures where the two people look at themselves, at their insides, while their eyes are hovering on the other's face: it was the tacit communication of orphanhood, the communion of a fact. A shared confrontation. They were missing someone, someone was missing them. The wind remarked sorrowfully on their absences.

Folding pieces of bread into a cloth napkin, the old woman explained to Verónica how it would be better for her to return with the help of the rope that they had strung through the trees to get to the road on a more comfortable path. Fénix drank a lot of water before they left the clearing, surrounded by the rhythmic barking of the dogs.

By now it was completely dark. The silence had also darkened in its way. They got to the edge of the road. She guessed the car was a few meters farther to the right. They advanced along the tree line, but there was no trace of the light that Verónica left as a kind of ostentatious trail of breadcrumbs. She thought she recognized the curb where she had pulled over, but there was nothing there. She was hit with the certainty that someone had taken the car, even though she had the keys. She went back into the forest, hoping that she had parked even farther in and that the battery had already died. At least she would have shelter. Fénix watched her, alert, from the grate of the cage, his pupils expanded in the lack of light. He meowed impatiently, letting her see his tiny animal canines.

She walked hurriedly toward the confirmation of her circumstances, forcing herself to look ahead. She stumbled over something and rolled, covering herself with the cold earth. The cage flew through the air, crashing to the ground a few meters ahead. When she could stand, she examined the bundle that had made her fall: a man with his head tilted, legs twisted at painful angles, arms inert at his sides. A mirror of black liquid shone beneath his abdomen and then grouped together in a broken ribbon, a long track climbing up to the road. Tire tracks.

The wet smell of earth mixed with the metallic scent of blood, making her want to vomit. She went toward the cage, where Fénix remained stunned, his head drooping. "My baby," she said. "Cat. Everything will be okay." She took him in her arms, petting his back. The animal, contrary to his usual behavior, let her do it. Once in a while, he turned his head and sniffed at her tears. When Verónica sobbed, the cat pushed his ears back and stared at her.

Every now and then, that tide-like wind picked up. But when it stopped and the atmosphere was calm, miniscule glimmers sprouted from the trees. Fireflies. Fénix opened his eyes wide, stepped forward a bit, retreated, aimed some tremulous warning growls. And then he simply enjoyed them.

"My mom calls fireflies 'cocuyos,' Fénix."

When the last one vanished, Fénix stretched with enthusiasm. He walked a bit farther and turned to see if Verónica was following. An impatient meow seemed to pressure her, as if at the mention of her mother, the cat decided that they should continue trying to get home. She rearranged Fénix and the little bit of food in the cage and got ready to walk, but the handle was broken. She wrapped what she could in her clothes and warned Fénix that he could let her carry him or walk with her without running off. The animal trotted ahead of her without talking back. Verónica noticed that she didn't feel the anguish of losing him again. She was certain, she *knew* it wouldn't happen. She accepted the idea that the end would sneak up on them as they walked in their noble attempt to get home. But before that, she left on the body of the stranger a little branch of velvety leaves she couldn't identify (she regretted not knowing the names of so many trees, so many plants). She did it because she remembered being taught in her history classes that humans became humans when they started to bury their dead with flowers and shrouds.

She sincerely hoped that man wasn't the son the woman was waiting for.

They walked a couple of hours without seeing anybody. Verónica kept moving on pure inertia. Fénix slept in her arms. Then a couple of cars appeared. She let the first two pass, hidden, as soon as she saw the headlights from afar. The third, which she didn't hide from, drove right by without even looking at her. The fourth was a pickup truck that stopped when it saw her.

"Where are you going?" they asked, and she didn't lie when she answered. "Come on. But leave that here," they said, referring to Fénix.

Verónica looked at the cat. Fénix looked at the strangers with the flaps of his nose flared.

"Then, no." Verónica kept walking, half of her chest filled with terror, the other half with a swell of sole determination.

The people in the truck stopped completely. They wanted to negotiate. They wouldn't let her leave. Verónica offered all the food that the old woman had given her in exchange for the presence of Fénix in the truck. They weren't interested in the cat's tubes of magic paste. She decided to try them during the trip. Fénix got sick on the way and meowed pitifully several times, provoking bitterness in some passengers and the curiosity of two girls who never stopped giggling; one older than the other, jolly as sleighbells.

Around midnight, they spotted the highway. From afar, it looked full, closed off in a dome of amber light. Verónica remembered the nightmare of the route that same morning. It seemed a remote and impossible past. She remembered the man with the tablet, the sight of that blinding darkness, advancing through the sky in a whirlwind. The truck continued to navigate the rocks of the unpaved road, advancing in parallel.

They arrived, finally and inevitably, to the main street of a town. The people seemed calmer here, despite the fact that the lights were out on some blocks. The man who sold bread and movies unscrewed the light that kept his rolls hot; two children ran ahead of their parents dragging some toy, lurching along behind them. Ladies with their heads covered tried to cross the street to the temple. It seemed everyone was going through a rarefied version of their Friday routine, that was all.

Verónica surmised that, if she kept going on foot along the edge of the road, she would arrive at the street that would take her home. It worried her not to take into account any impossible-to-walk drops or distances that, in a car, she'd always ignored. But she decided to run the risk. She was able to get to where the municipal highway started, barely able to distinguish it in the dark earth, even though in the sky there was, when the clouds dispersed, a light pinkish glow.

Verónica looked to it constantly. The stars shone sharply, closely. For a time she thought she imagined flickers in the sky because of the optical illusions of fireflies, who were still accompanying her. But yes: up there, in who knows what secret code, the lights blinked and moved. They went dark or glowed. Her fingers settled nervously in Fénix's fur. If she stopped for a moment, her feet twinged with an unbearable burning, functioning as an alert of proximity connected to the ground, and she couldn't tear her eyes away from the sky: above and below they encouraged her not to stop, like the enchanted girl in the story about the red shoes who never stopped dancing.

Houses started appearing little by little and in clusters in the neighborhood near her parents'. There was still a labyrinthian stretch of improvised streets and unpaved roads. The wind strengthened in freezing swells that contrasted with the warmth emanated by the walls, with the breathing of the trees. She found some of the doors in the housing complex wide open, rendering useless the alarm codes, the keys, and the spiked gates that in another time the neighbors had deemed indispensable.

Everyone was waiting for someone. That's why anyone could come in now. The nausea that she got at the thought of finding nothing, nobody, vanished when she made out the silhouettes of her parents. Verónica could distinguish every one of her relatives from the highest point of the slope that led cars to the houses farther back. She saw her sister who, like a reflection turning its back, looked up without attending to the child who was tugging at her sweater sleeve. The lights in the sky unraveled into multiple colors that turned in diminutive spirals, tiny fireworks, and nobody did anything but celebrate them in silent astonishment.

The family camped in the living room with the curtains open to keep watching the spectacle. They closed their eyes every now and again. There were conversations between pairs and others where everyone participated. The tides of wind were the only causes of breaks in this unexpected rejoicing. Fénix went in and out of the backyard, threw himself for a while on Verónica's stomach, then lurked in the doorway, sniffing the faces of people who were sleeping, which earned him a few whacks. But he didn't stop watching. Verónica found him stopping for long periods of time on the children's faces.

Only the two of them were still awake when a flock of birds came down from the sky, singing loudly. The clocks read nine in the morning, but the sky was dark, splashed with the luminous coloring of the spirals, which were close now. Turquoise, lilac, yellow, pale green. They were beautiful. The freezing gusts of wind occurred more frequently like the progressive accelerations of contractions before birth.

Fénix kept watch on the windowsill, leering threateningly at the birds. One of them, a bluish-black rook, hopped onto the cornice, looking between the two of them with one eye and then the other.

The spirals approached more and more quickly. In a subtle progression, things started to lift. Verónica recognized in those liquid colors the nothing that consumed everything from that video the man in the street had tried to show them. It was this, not a blinding darkness that she had seen. Nevertheless, it felt so different ...

The birds let out a series of disparate, elevated sounds. The wind began its rounds again. A pealing began, soft and distant, musical. The video camera that captured the phenomenon had no eyes, sense of touch, ears that functioned by the mysterious mechanisms of living beings. Maybe that's why it wasn't able to capture the marvel that Fénix saw, too, that the bird perceived as well with its beak raised to the stars.

Water, there was a sweet rushing of hidden water behind the window. Its part in the music also intensified. Time stretched on one harmonic note.

People leaned out. They looked at each other. They helped each other explain that phrase which repeated over and over in the air.

The cat looked at Verónica. She recognized in his face, so familiar and yet so distant, the affection that they had built together over the years. She also learned a secret, a cipher that defined her there inside of his yellow eyes. Fénix recognized his cat face in the girl's dark pupil, and his joy was the same as that of the bird, and that of everyone who, looking around, found each other at last in the mirror, less and less distant from the spirals, from the music, from the end of the party.

LA PURIFICACIÓN

In the middle of the night, a suffocating feeling wakes me. The air is so hot that my thighs are slippery with sweat. The man I loved is by my side with his back to me. I know that I can't go to him, that I have to live this anguish and this horror alone and that he is right to turn his face from me. I hear rainfall and thank the heavens: I hope the water is freezing, I hope it stays a while, I hope it extinguishes this hell's mouth. The rain, however, does not answer my prayers. I hear it come and go, alternating with some familiar-sounding footsteps. I get up. There must be someone lurking around here.

Through the window I see it's not raining. Someone is watering the plants, the little trees that I and the man I loved planted a while ago in an attempt to add some green to our house. They're almost dry now. He's been caring for them, tending them more than I have, but it's not enough to bring them back to life. The shadow I see through the window looks like the man I loved, but it's not him. He's in bed where I left him, mulling over his dream of fury and sorrow. As I get closer, I hear the shadow drag its feet while watering the leaves, the branches, and the rhythm of the steps tells me who it is before I see her hair, her hands, her face. It's my grandmother.

"You remind me of my grandmother, but I'm not sure why," I've said to him many times. He would just laugh and caress my face. And then I realized why he reminded me of her.

My grandmother sprays water over the soil, picks up a broom, and starts to scrub briskly as she always did. Then she douses the mud with the water left in the basin, a little aluminum box that looks new even though I haven't seen it since I was a child.

"Gran!" I say with frenzied affection. "Granny." I hug her, kiss her hair, alabaster curls that smell like orange blossoms.

"Sweetheart," she says. "Look how careless you've been. They're going to die."

"They are dying. I don't know how to stop it."

"You do know. But you don't want to." As always, my grandmother is right.

"What are you doing here, crazy lady?"

"I'm out with your aunt to meet with a friend. Come with me since I've already scared you awake."

I don't even know where she's taking me. We walk down the streets that surround my house, but suddenly I don't know them. I'm like a blind dog. I walk with her like I have a fever and a veil of smoke over my eyes. We go pretty far, all the way to the town where she was born, to La Purificación. I recognize this road lined by myrtles, the hill that leads to the cemetery, the atrium outside the church. There are no night watchmen, not one trace of life in the street. Maybe it's because it's only dawn, I think. My sweat keeps consuming me, as if I were a melting candle made of flesh.

"But it never gets this hot here. Remember how, every time we spent the night here, we had to get an extra blanket out from the linen closet?" I say to my grandmother.

She doesn't answer.

The street going out of town, the one with the pretty gates, is darker than I remember. The dogs are barking at the red door of Aunt Concha's house, which I know is red because I remember it, not because I see it. I don't see the dogs either.

"Concha! Open up! I'm here with the girl!"

"The girl." Gran, I'm an adult now. Though I've been so bad, so bad ...

I realize that I'm hungry. On Aunt Concha's table there will be hot buns and refried beans, I'm certain. My aunt emerges from the shadows of the house, dodging affectionate leaps from the invisible dogs. She takes the largest key from her key ring and opens the door. Her rosy-cheeked face shines as much as the lenses in her glasses, which obscure her eyes.

"The girl!" exclaims my aunt, and she hugs me. "Come in. We're making bread."

From the window I can see the dining room inside the house. Tall lamps illuminate the glassware, the tablecloth, the dishes: a party of white, gold, and red. I want to sit at the table, which is already set, but my aunt and grandmother head straight to the back patio. I feel the dogs' happy tails thumping my legs, but I don't see them. The vision of the house's interior has dazzled me, and I still have a cloud of warm sleep over my eyes.

The little door of the stone oven is open. Bricks are burning inside, brilliant like the red-orange that spurts from volcanic fissures, where the earth's belly has purged itself. Once I dreamed I gave birth to a pile of stones, which should have been pure heat, since they were alive. But they came out cold, inert, damp. They would be useless for baking bread.

Thinking about that dream convinces me that I'm not dreaming this.

My Aunt Concha points at a large table covered in flour. Beside the freshly-made, shapeless dough lies a tray covered with steaming loaves of bread that turned out a bit charred. In the sky above, a few stars twinkle indecisively.

"Make your dolls, darling. And don't forget to put a cross on them, so they'll be blessed."

"Gran, it's not November 2nd, yet. Why are you making pan de muerto?"

She doesn't respond. My Aunt Concha is the one who answers:

"Because you came."

I make three loaves: one in the shape of a tree, one in the shape of a man, another in the shape of a woman. They turn out big and pretty. I place them on the peel and slide them into the oven. I feel as if I'm melting when I lean toward the little fire. Now I have to wait.

"Gran, I'm hungry."

My grandmother kisses me, pinches my cheek, just like before, when we played like we were little friends and I was a huge nuisance. But before, she would have offered me something to eat without a second thought.

Not anymore.

"In a bit. As soon as the dough is cooked, I'll take you back."

I want to tell her that I'd like to sit inside the house, in the dining room, that I'm craving queso fresco and hot coffee, but my granny and aunt are motionless, sitting outside, receiving a visitor. Doloritas, they call her. She came from far away, they have to catch up. They talk among themselves in a murmur that at first seems unintelligible, like when I was a kid and didn't understand the chatting of grown-ups. They share the burnt bread. They dip it in their coffee, they eat it. The smell of anise makes my mouth water. When I reach out to take a small piece, my grandmother smacks my hand away. As a kid I would have complained, but I say nothing because I missed her fingers, wide and crooked from arthritis, covered with bronze and brass rings. I take her hand and caress it. I get the strong urge to cry because she's been dead for so many years and I know that she can't smack me or talk to me or hug me afterwards when I'm so sad because the trees dried up and the man I loved sinks into the bed until he disappears without looking at me twice, like a slab of pumice stone submerged in a deep river, so defeated. And it's all my fault.

Little by little, I start to understand what their whispering means. Aunt Concha is talking about how annoying her dogs are, Doloritas is talking about the unfinished business she has with her son. Doña Pola talks about baptisms and funerals, about how she always has to be the godmother of christening gowns and shrouds. It's difficult to follow them. They say so many things, all important, all detached from the angry and sad world of men. I stop listening when my eye catches the fiery border that seals the oven closed, my breads burning inside it like bodies burn in a crematorium. I lose myself in the red halo until I realize that the three women are talking to me, their faces turned toward me.

"It's hard to accept the end of things."

"It's not your fault. You haven't been so bad, so bad. You're just bored to death."

They laugh.

"It's worse when you don't accept the end because it creates a limbo. A perpetual gloom."

"A girl could get trapped there. Or here, forever."

"To each her own, if she's dead anyway."

"But you're alive."

"And while there is life, the sun always rises."

"Always."

The air is filled with brown sugar and anise, the sweetness of bread. Doloritas helps me open the oven door and take out, one by one, the breads they had also put in to bake. They're shaped like dogs, houses, horses, children.

And there will be a party soon. Beneath the stars I can just see a procession of cheerful little lanterns coming down the hill toward the cemetery. I understand that my perfect bread, unburnt, is for them: food for souls in limbo. I can't eat the beans or the toasted buns. Aunt Concha's table isn't set for me.

"The girl knows, Pola. Let her go."

"But you all have to come with me to her door. So she doesn't feel alone."

"All right then. Let's go."

I walk with the three women at my side. They are much stronger than I am. They don't struggle to breathe, and they don't sweat, even when we make it to the atrium in the blink of an eye.

"You can still run out of breath. Enjoy it. We don't need it anymore," says one of them, or the three (I don't know, it's hard to be sure) with sage acceptance.

The air is fresh, maybe because the sun is coming up here in this place we've come to. I spot the door of my house. Aunt Concha, Doloritas, and Doña Pola stand stiffly in the threshold, though I invite them to come in. I suppose they can't, and this is where I have to leave them.

I cling to my grandmother even though I'm afraid that she'll crumble, that she's made of flour and orange blossom water. But she latches onto me like she did when her body was living, when there was no danger in the world that could reach me as long as she was holding my hand.

When I open my eyes, with the sun hitting me square in the face, I discover that I am finally sleeping alone, hugging my own body, surrounded by breadcrumbs.

Future Nereid

Now you can't determine when you started to search for him; when you repeated his name in a soft voice or where you were the first time the preoccupied brush of your hand through the hair at the nape of your neck warned you that you loved him.

You can, however, remember when you realized that he lived in the world—like you—and the image comes to you, luminous and long, a golden cord that someone extends to you down into the abyss. You remember that you will knock at the door and Ricardo will let you in. Everyone will be drinking beer, but you didn't feel like it. You drank a glass of agua fresca with crushed mint while listening to the cheerful drumroll of the party.

Someone will throw out a question (maybe the lost genealogy of a Greek hero), and another asked you to answer it, which you did truthfully and humbly.

How do you know so much, Nerissa?

This girl will read anything, even the back of the cereal box. Ask her anything, and with every word spoken by that horde of unwitting fools, you will long even more for the soothing company of books.

Ricardo warned you, under the pretext of needing your help, he'll take you from the circle, bring you to a closet filled with papers, books, and relics. In that little room you felt comfortable at last. You'll observe the foreign hands of your friend adjust, dust off, catalogue pieces and pages on one of his little portable screens. You thought of all those people who live from move to move until, in some remote place, with every trace of their past life gone, they find peace.

But you weren't born in the wrong place, just the wrong time. How can you settle down when it's impossible to move? Pick out what you want to take home this week, Ricardo's friendly voice offers, to compensate for the embarrassment. You asked for the book with green edges and silvery lettering. You'll protect it in the rush of handbags and subway cars, pore over the index through eyelashes braided by astigmatism, and will choose page 23.

Umbrarium is the name of the story. You were very moved. You noticed the initials that disguised the name of the author: *P.M.* You got out of the car, will go to your house feeling the universe of the story inhabit you, the air transformed by the pages in an aching, gentle weight in your chest.

(Umbrarium, page 26):

It isn't that I, in the simple transit of my life, have never found a virtuous woman. On the contrary, I have admired the strength of female friends and the beauty of passersby; I have contemplated gestures at length, laughed along with ingenuous voices; even modesty does not impede me from remembering that I have loved the touch of shapes and warmths. Still, nobody before has submerged me in the depths of the purest love as she did. The Nereid ...

You'll love the story of the Nereid, not just because of the closeness to your own name, but also because of the water carried by that word and creature. You'll read certain passages more than once, soaking in the tub, walking in the shallow end of the pool where you exercised, on the table by the fountain you escape to during dinner. You will return the book apprehensively, you wondered whether this would be one you had to take by force, you thought about saying to Ricardo: *Give it to me, it's not yours. Please.* But sense will return to your head, and like the good girl you will be, you returned it; and like the good girl you are, you will ask in a timid voice in every bookstore on that street—this one here is called Montealegre—if they had, anywhere, the story of the umbrarium. You'll describe it with wide eyes, the green edges, the silver letters ... nothing.

Many dawns passed when you thought of his words threaded like crystals, or bells, or silk flowers.

(Umbrarium, page 28):

Eroded like a rock on the cliff always struck by the cruelest waves, I put an end to the difficult transit between one love and another. I was sick of feeling out of place; scorned for showing women (maids, widows, or girls) a respect uncommon of men of my time. While they wondered which mares or furniture formed part of their dowries, I longed for a companion with whom I could talk about all of this in the most indignant tone, with whom to dialogue as equals, enduring together the pain of the present, giving each other hope in some situation to come ...

Later, you'll get out of bed mid-insomnia, feeling stupid for not having typed those initials into the database. At a first glance you'll think the only results were covers of dull, out-of-print books. Diving a bit deeper, you found a trail of knowledgeable informants, your breath getting closer and closer to the screen. You will find the name and a brief biography: Pascal Marsias, a peculiar character in the country's cultural life in the nineteenth century, born in the same city as you. Author of scarce, late publication, whose core themes are love and fantasy: journeys through time and space. His work consists of a few stories published in newspapers, magazines of the time, some anthologies (the one that you read stood out as the most recent), and a book of poems: *Songs for a Future Nereid*. He disappeared, nobody knows how or when.

As if the shock weren't enough, your finger finds the button that displays images. You'll touch it hastily. Suddenly, a photograph. You felt a drumbeat in the veins of your wrist when the screen was filled with him: a miniature in charcoal showing a man like any other, but in his face you saw his words reverberate, in his lips that you touched by mere impulse you found delirium, because they seemed tremendously familiar. You wondered if what you were perceiving was an echo of something still unspoken; if the future could, at times, be impatient, show itself imprudently in the now. You rejected the idea immediately, and you will decide you're being stupid. In your belly something will shrink when you think of the unfortunate distance that at times separates us from souls so akin to our own.

(Umbrarium, page 31)

The sensation became more urgent when I reviewed my travel diaries. Paradoxically, I was not yet capable of controlling my will because all it wanted was to be close to her. So I became dedicated to completing her, drawing her on paper like a character in my stories: what would please her, how her movements would be, what kind of friends would surround her. Beneath what horizon? It seemed distant, remote, like my journeys to the ulterior, but in any case, that night in the umbrarium, for one moment I saw her face ...

You adored the writing of Pascal Marsias for many reasons. But above all, you'll say, you loved that compassionate gaze, the discussion of humanity lying in the story. What seemed like the story of an arrogant man, so desperate from not finding a worthy wife that—like Pygmalion—he decides to construct his own, in reality was a beautiful defense of love, emphasized by its final lines:

I thought that there was no point in building The Nereid. If there was anything that needed to be created, it was the world that would make it possible. Since then I have done my part, trying to be a good man who gives to others the virtue that lives in him.

Good love, a good that just worlds deserve, you thought. You would have liked to underline the entire book in substitution for a series of caresses.

The next day you'll call in. You said, *I won't go, no real reason, I'm coming down with the flu, and I don't want to make anyone sick.* The metro would be the cradle of your desire, the swaying of a longing that made your most ordinary gestures adorable. The air from the open window will bring the black threads of your hair to your mouth, you'll wet them with your saliva, a gesture close to a kiss. The wind, too, that strange burst, will scatter the papers of the lady clinging to the tube. You picked them up because you are kind.

The center boiled beneath your steps because you'll have that hang-up about covering your feet, even though the spring had already announced itself in violets and yellows. You noticed the clear sky, you will breathe in the coolness of March air, feeling over you the serene embrace of the present. You'll look through every shelf, entering, leaving disheveled and rosy from the street—whose name has changed—a damsel on Donceles Street, one volume, another, another, dampness, dust, sawdust, ink, leather, parchment, your weak fingers will tug at your lower lip, and you'll say, *Can you look for something else by this author?* And your coral-colored mouth sketched peaches in the air when you pronounced his name. But nobody found him.

You became dispirited. Until, turning onto a hot white corner, you saw that small bookstore removing its padlocks, opening its rusted gate. You'll walk to it without hesitation, let out a huff of surprise when you discover that the tiny door leads to high walls covered with enormous bookcases, the books like a miraculous infestation. You'll look at the labels stuck on with transparent tape, feel the pulse of the words creep up your arm. You didn't want to ask for help; finding him on your own was the prize. And you did it: two shelves above you was your book, living its life of solitary longing, *Songs for a Future Nereid*.

You trembled. You'll pay with a translucent bill, they'll take a while to give you the change, but you didn't open the cloth cover. You'll want to wait, but for what? You couldn't say, but you preferred it that way. You'll feel a wave of gratitude because you knew that moment had a mark, as if someone had placed a silver separator between the pages. You'll know that this moment brought you here.

Nerissa! You heard the flutter of your name in the street, a beloved and familiar voice. You'll turn … Ricardo, who shouted at you several times, and you did nothing. You didn't notice. *Do you know Pascal Marsias?* you ask in despair. *I don't think so*. You looked at him sadly. And you omitted what you had to omit, but you will tell Ricardo about him.

The Spindle of the Golden Cord (page 10)

The thread of the fates wastes no metal
I discovered it last night, in the umbrarium
made of aroma, shirts turned inside out
Generous thread of time, traveler
Life is your destiny, future or past
I saw in that false laudanum dream
what Dante's madness never could

because it was not the vast expanse of hell
but my secret longings
with their exposed entrails
The solitude of that familiar house
—in the middle of the night the candle and me—
my juvenile sex in the lake, the trees
I saw my father ...

You will realize the point of the book of poems. You read one time that it had to do with *speculative fiction in verse*; but seeing it, the frayed seams, the smell—always that smell of lime and dusty perfume—you knew immediately that it was a toolkit, a kind of formula. For some reason you remembered those old witchcraft books ("legs of a spider, tail of a dragon"), you'll notice that the written instructions were precise, though their results were uncertain.

So you'll know that there were tailors who ended up having tea in their childhood homes when they fastened their buttons backwards and girls who witnessed the resurgence of an empire when they folded socks. As always, you feared confusing life with a book, and the mere thought that all those things were true made your chest feel tight. Is that true, you'll wonder, with the naivete of someone who has never read a lie, hand resting on your forehead. You'll mix his name with an empty sigh in the air. You looked in the mirror, wishing it was him looking back. You laughed at these things just so you wouldn't feel completely crazy.

You arrived at the final collection of verses. The soft hairs on the back of your neck will stand on end in a feline gesture, and a few lines ahead you'll get a strange chill. You'll find what you were looking for in the final poem.

Song for Future Nereid (page 42):

A painful idea,
I wanted to see the future, my blind faith in the future

I saw the ash-colored future of my home,
Porcelain stained by feasts of mud,
I saw Montealegre Street filled with trains people
lights all incomprehensible.
And I saw you.
Nereid reborn, close and Apollonian
I saw you move
inhabit the air with goodness and grace
You carried something in your body that I had lost
it shined bright as a jewel pinned in your hair
Somebody called you Nerissa
(Nerissa, like you, this afternoon, and the street, and Ricardo)
and in the simple consonance of your name
I understood that it was you the missing and recovered.
Come, future Nereid
find our invisible connection
scent trails or sundials
Go without fear for one thing is certain:
the umbrarium lies in wait
to shelter us again.

You thought about burning the book, just like in the old days when they burned witchcraft books, and torn between panic and wonder you'll hide in the corner of your bed. There is no possible misunderstanding: it's you. The book was talking to you, or you are deranged.

What blessed blindness will make you choose the former?

Half-dressed, you'll go to Ricardo, who will say I'm glad you came over, even though it's a little late. You took the book, coming up with dumb lies. *An essay to write, it's due tomorrow, you need* this *book to finish it.*

Where to go? What station do all the impossible trains leave from? You were so used to stories where there's a big machine with schedules and levers and buttons that you won't be able to think straight. But you'll be cunning: you realized that this was less science and more sorcery. You'll decide that the place where the witches are safest is their own house. You went to the shelter asking for a stray cat for company, just in case.

You'll revisit over and over the pages of the volumes written by Pascal Marsias. The touch screen will stain with the silky marks of your digital fingerprints. You'll look time and again for any kind of formula (botanical, mathematical, mechanical) to turn back time. No useful way will come to you. You will touch the sensitive outline of your lips, knowing yourself loved across some kind of gap. You cried at the cruel nature of your love, your human insignificance. And at the same time, gratitude, a certain sympathy for all versions of life that took form in your bones, your flesh, your scent. It was then that you achieved the victory of all lovers: you got up, sniffled through tears walking toward the desk where the notebook and pen lay, and you will start to write:

Dancers have the key in the movement of their bodies; birds, magnetizing the air with their beaks. Me? It's not just a matter of knowing the way. To discover it, you have to know who you are. Who are you, Nerissa?

A heap of answers come to mind from centuries of pages and pages, but you will find it difficult to think of one for yourself.

Who am I?

On the paper, you began to slide the ink like thick black blood. Brilliant and definitive, you'll write:

I am Nerissa. I swim and read. I believe in the impossible worlds imagined by people, in the unspoken truth of books, the life of stories. More and more, I believe that I myself am part of one. I am Nerissa, I am the future nereid. And Pascal Marsias made the necessary world so that I could live. I write these lines so that the words and my body combine into the perfect machine ...

Here you'll stop because, in the corner of your eye, you saw something move. You didn't notice that all the shadows of the world shifted to the opposite side, but the tingle in your stomach will make you continue.

I want to go to him, to the exact moment he's waiting for me. I know it's possible because it's already happened. In one thread of time the journey has been made.

Your mirror will reflect other walls, other light, enormous leaves, and the roof woven with vines emitting sweet, earthy scents. You avoided moving for fear of undoing whatever was happening.

Because he, Pascal Marsias, has seen me in the umbrarium.

And while the vertigo of Time tosses you in its abysmal current, I, Pascal Marsias, set my pen and the manuscript of your story aside, for I see you appear next to me, dear Nerissa, here, in the umbrarium.

Retreat from the
World Outside

Let us imagine a being, invested with such knowledge, to examine at a distant epoch the coincidence of the facts with those which his profound analysis had enabled him to predict. If any the slightest deviation existed, he would immediately read in its existence the action of a new cause ... The air itself is one vast library, on whose pages are for ever written all that man has ever said or woman whispered. There, in their mutable but unerring characters, mixed with the earliest, as well as with the latest sighs of mortality, stand for ever recorded, vows unredeemed, promises unfulfilled, perpetuating in the united movements of each particle, the testimony of man's changeful will.

Charles Babbage

Most Reverend Fathers, Assessors of the Holy Office Brother Fernando Loera and Brother Alberto de Mendoza:

By order of the Tribunal, I submit to Your Reverences the following objects so that you may present the assessment and penitence which falls to you:

—Notes handwritten by the nun Sister Ágata de la Luz of the convent of Corpus Christi of Mexico for Noble Indians, found in her cell.

—An artifact, possibly produced by the nun herself, of function and use unknown, perhaps heretical, also found in her cell.

—A plate or disc of clay, found with the artifact.

The objects were confiscated from the cell of the nun following accusations from Sister María Devota del Niño Jesús, another nun at the convent of Corpus Christi, who describes Sister Ágata de la Luz as deluded, bewitched, and heretical, as well as guilty of having committed acts of fornication with another accused heretic who will have his own justice, Father Alfonso de Alba.

May God guide Your Reverend Fathers to enact a pious and just sentence, Our Holy Inquisition in Mexico, January of 1779.

Alonso López, Secretary.

Statement of Sister Elena, gatekeeper

Sister Elena de la Concepción, of Veracruz, declares herself the gatekeeper of the convent of Corpus Christi for eight years, describes her position as "responsible for receiving, through the window and the turnstile, everything which enters and exits the convent, including the people who frequent it: the bricklayer, the doctor, the barber, relatives of the nuns, the bishops, the surgeon, the blessed, the gardener ..." When asked whether Father Alfonso de Alba had visited the convent, she said yes. When asked whether his visits were frequent, she said yes. When asked if he specifically visited Sister Ágata, she again said yes, but added that this was not out of the ordinary, considering that Father de Alba is Sister Ágata's confessor. When asked whether these visits were made late at night, she firmly said no, the turnstile closes at five o'clock in the evening, she is very vigilant of her office and schedule, and in addition Father de Alba is a pious man, by all accounts. When shown the artifact and the plate found in Sister Ágata's cell and asked when these items had entered the convent, she was very quiet. She claimed having no memory of these objects entering the cloister. Sister Elena would not look up after answering this question.

Statement of Sister Francisca, provisor

Sister Francisca de la Cruz, born in Tlatelolco, Mexico, declares herself the provisor of the convent for fifteen years. She proceeded to describe her tasks, very proud to carry them out as pleases the Lord: "responsible for stocking the cupboards with everything necessary to feed the sisters, making sure the table is set for daily meals, that is to say, giving each nun her mat, napkin, water, cutlery, fruit and bread, serving hot chocolate twice a day; and maintaining the condition of the books that the Subprioress reads out loud as everyone eats," among other obligations. She was asked whether she noticed what Sister María Devota had described in the previous days, that there were utensils missing from the kitchen, to which she answered no. She was asked to show the inventory of cutlery and flatware, which she did without hesitation. She compared the written inventory with the pieces, revealing the missing ones, to which the nun, surprised, declared that she had not yet noticed, since she had just finished the inventory. She was shown the artifact found in Sister Ágata's quarters and was asked if she recognized the missing piece (a napkin ring) as one of its components. Sister Francisca, looking carefully at the artifact, said that she did not. Nonetheless, the fathers conducting the investigation identified a piece of brass which may have been part of the napkin ring and brought it to the nun's attention. She shrugged her shoulders and said that she could not, based on this piece, be sure that Sister Ágata had stolen the napkin ring, and that to her, the accused nun was "a jewel of the convent: sweet, obedient, and very understanding," not like "Sister María Devours," and having spoken this nickname she covered her mouth in shame and had to confess that this is what they called her in the convent because they were all decent Indian caciques while Maria was creole, but with bad will toward her sisters. Then she offered everyone present some cooked snacks with the image of Saint Teresa that Sister Rosa had made that morning and explained that they had been blessed, specifically, by Father Alfonso.

Statement of Juana, slave of Sister María Devota

Juana Dolores, mulatta daughter of a black slave, was given by her confessor and relative Brother Eusebio Figueroa (Spanish, benefactor of the convent of Corpus Christi) to Sister María Devota when she joined the convent. The tasks she carries out for the nun are typical: she cleans her bedchambers, organizes her clothes and belongings, "which," she explained, "despite being a nun are those of a lady of her station," takes her messages and runs her errands outside of the convent, and undergoes the nun's corporal tasks if she is sick or indisposed, which occurs frequently.

Juana was asked whether she had witnessed Sister María Devota's spiritual raptures, which include: having seen the Virgin Mary cutting roses in the garden, perceiving the holy scent of the corpse of Saint Teresa de Ávila during a mass, sprouting a wound in her side like the one of Christ, preparing meals and washing dishes with the assistance of the Baby Jesus, having drunk milk from the breasts of the Virgin Mary. At the last anecdote, Juana seemed on the verge of laughter, but she contained herself and stated that if this was what her lady had said, then that was what she, too, had seen.

Then she was asked if she had witnessed the offenses attributed to Sister Ágata, and answered no. She was scolded again, since María Devota had said herself that she sent her slave to observe the activities of Sister Ágata's at night, fearing for the state of her soul. Juana said that her lady María had indeed sent her to Ágata's bedchambers, but that she had seen nothing, only heard voices. When asked whose voices she heard, she said that they were the voices of other nuns.

This was the night Ágata had been excused from attending mass and from Compline because she had fallen ill. She had heard many voices coming from behind the door, she wouldn't be able to say how many nuns, and the voices were speaking and singing. The slave Juana claimed not to know which songs these were, but she did know that they were sung in Mexican languages, given that all of the nuns, minus her lady, are Indians, and speak their own languages when they are alone. She also said that they were very lovely songs, like lullabies to calm the child God. Juana declared that she told just this to Sister María Devota, who took it badly, "perhaps because they didn't invite her." Then her lady ordered her to report the incident to the Prioress so that she would reprimand them, which Juana did right away. But when the Prioress entered Ágata's bedchambers, there was nobody there with her, and she could not be reprimanded, which infuriated her lady, who wanted to see them punished.

At the question of whether she believed Sister María Devota had fabricated the accusations against Sister Ágata, Juana responded, without raising her eyes from the ground, that "what her lady says is how it must be." At the question of whether she considered Sister María to be a mystic, she once again held back a smile and responded that she did not know because, as her lady says, she is "black and ignorant and foolish."

Description of the artifact found in Sister Ágata's cell

Presented to the Tribunal of the Holy Office is an object of many assembled pieces: a small wooden box with an exterior handle which allows its operation, repurposed from a chili pepper grinder. On the box are attached the following pieces: a small paper cone similar to the pointed hats and hoods worn on the heads of those condemned by the Holy Office, except that its end is not pointed but wrapped, at its thinnest end, around a frame used for embroidery. Instead of thread, the frame has fixed to it the skin of an animal (pig or calf), so thin that it vibrates with the simple movement of the air. Before this membrane stands an iron shaft upright on the box. At its end is a pivot made of brass (likely repurposed from the lost napkin ring), which holds a thick needle with no point like a sewing needle cut down. And in front of the tip of this needle, the apparatus has a wooden disc, arranged vertically, which turns when the handle is manipulated (likely a repurposed potter's wheel on which ceramic is molded). In its center stand two bronze pegs, perhaps to support a disc made of another material. Prior to the statement of Sister Ágata, Brother Severino, scholar of mathematics and physics, was consulted as to what the function of such a machine could be.

Statement and intervention of Brother Servino de Segovia

Brother Servino, of Sevilla, Spain, belongs to the order of Saint Francis and lived first in Mérida before residing in Mexico, where he is an instructor at the Royal and Pontifical University. When examining the artifact, Brother Servino put his ear to the cone, then his mouth, then spoke and shouted into it. Then he asked a student who was accompanying him to do the same. He observed the behavior of the membrane and the needle while this happened. Brother Severino moved the handle on multiple occasions, using different amounts of force, which accelerated and decelerated the movement of the wooden disc. He then took a measurement of the space between the disc and the needle and asked the Tribunal to provide the clay disc found with the artifact. He secured it easily to the wooden disc, bending the brass pegs in its center, thereby discovering the function of the pegs. But he did not turn the handle, declaring that if he were to do so, the clay disc would hit the needle and shatter. Then he removed the disc. He scratched his chin and left to eat, leaving his student walking circles around the apparatus, confused, for a duration of roughly two hours.

Upon his return Brother Severino put his nose to the wooden disc and asked his student to do the same. "What does it smell like?" he asked.

The student, timid, returned the question. "What does it smell like to you, professor?"

Brother Severino rolled his eyes and exclaimed that it plainly smelled of the Tepezcohuite tree. The father ordered a servant to ask the provisor what the nuns bathed themselves with and to return with a sample of the soap.

After a time, the servant arrived with the answer: twice a year they solicited from the soap manufactory in the city a certain quantity of bars of soap like the one which in this moment she delivered to the father. Brother Severino sniffed at the sample, smiled in satisfaction, and gave it to his student, who looked at him with admiration.

The father asked all present to place the disc close to their noses, then the bar, and at the affirmation that they both smelled of the Tepezcohuite tree he agreed, proud of his findings, though the rest of the room were not quite sure of what all of this meant. Brother Severino sent for the provisor, asking her additionally for the books where the orders of soap from the manufactory were logged.

After a time, the provisor brought the list. The father, analyzing the accounts of bars of soap in the previous months, determined that the soap orders had increased considerably in the last three months. On interrogating the provisor for the reason, she said that it was due to, of course, the spring, "that the air this year was quite hot and the humors of the sisters, therefore, more abundant." Immediately thereafter, the provisor and the servants brought the officials soft candies, quinces, snacks made of almond and cinnamon. But this did not deter Brother Severino, who, with his mouth full of sweets, proceeded to explain the following conclusions:

—That the artifact was crafted by the nun with various pieces from her own cell (the grinder, the sewing needle with no point, the frame), purchased and brought as contraband and/or stolen from the convent's common areas (the pig or calf skin, the potter's wheel, the brass piece). This would constitute, if proven, an additional crime.

—That the apparatus in question employed knowledge of mechanics as well as acoustics: the presence of the cone and the membrane uphold this. Its intention seems to be to replicate the human ear, whether it be an object to study its mechanisms or to improve its function, for example, to alleviate the effects of deafness, in the best of cases.

—That the artifact is, seemingly, a product of the nun's ingenuity, an extraordinary thing, although she was certainly assisted by a man, because such a task would require complex readings in the science of anatomy, acoustics, and mechanics, some of which are even banned by the Holy Office. Volumes like these do not exist in the Convent for Noble Indians of Corpus Christi, but only in the libraries of certain schools and libraries, where the fathers can use them (in many instances with prior censorship or explicit permission), and in universities.

—That the nun must have used clay discs like the one found in her cell to carry out her first attempts, but for some reason they were not satisfactory. Therefore, using her supply of Tepezcohuite tree soap, she molded a disc from this material so that the needle could make circular marks while the disc spun with the turning of the handle. The purpose of these circular marks would remain uncertain until the completion of an experiment that tested this function of the machine on the part of Brother Severino, as well as the statement of Sister Ágata de la Luz regarding its purpose.

Statement of Ofelia del Monte, servant

Ofelia, an Indian of Oaxaca, affirms that she has worked as a servant at the orders of Sister Paula de la Ascención, clothier of the convent, "who is also an Indian from Oaxaca. I say this, and I hope you will write it down just as I've said it, because it is important in order to understand certain matters regarding Sister María Devota, with all due respect," she established at the beginning of her statement, for which reason it was made sure that her words were collected exactly as she pronounced them in the following paragraphs:

"Sister Paula and the Prioress, the provisor, the accountant, and in brief, all of the nuns and servants of the convent lived in peace and harmony because the decision was made to make a space for those of us women with natural origins in Mexico, and in all of New Spain, since it is undeniable that we are treated differently for having dark skin. Though some of us are descended from great Mexican lordships, we suffer a great deal of mistreatment, in God's honest truth.

"Well, this harmony ended with the arrival of Sister María, imposed by a benefactor of the convent who is, additionally, a man of dubious repute. I am only saying, I have no desire to conspire or to offend because I am, after all, a simple servant. With the pardon of Your Reverences, I will say that, no matter what we do, Sister María devours us with her eyes, and her appetite for gossip and rumors is never satisfied. I say this with all due respect, but she watches constantly to see if a nun has done this or failed to do that in order to report her to the superiors and gain their favor, or that is how it appears, though I repeat, I have no judgement.

"Unlike the rest of us, among whom, thanks to the sisters' good hearts, there is little distinction between servants, slaves, and holy women, Mother María always tells us that there is an order of castes to respect, as if we were enemies of disorder (which we are not) and above all, she shows disgust at what she calls 'the humors of the dark-skinned' when she turns in her clothing, always making sure that her garments are not mixed with the rest.

"She makes a face of disgust if we talk amongst ourselves in our languages from Oaxaca or Yucatan or Mexico, but because this is a convent for Indians the superiors give us the right and permission, which does not please her and gives rise to her fantasies, such as that we are invoking our ancient demons or similar lies. She is said to be a mystic, but the superiors of the convent know that her raptures, like her many illnesses, are caused more by her hunger for attention than anything else. Anyone who tries to be more devout or more favored in the grace of God than she is will face accusations from her like the ones she is making today against Sister Ágata. This is what I say, and if you'd like, I will sign it, although I cannot write, because my conscience is calm and my soul in the hands of God and the Virgin Mary of Guadalupe, forgive me the boldness of telling this truth."

Statement of Father Alfonso de Alba

Brother Alfonso de Alba, of Mexico, declares himself the confessor of Sister Ágata for five years, since her previous confessor died, the much-respected Father Máximo de Legazpi, who believed it appropriate to pass down the task to him given that Brother Alfonso and Sister Ágata had known each other since their early childhood, before she had retreated from the outside world and he had been ordained.

At the question of whether he had heard Sister Ágata's confession more often than recommended by the Holy See (twice or three times a year), Brother Alfonso responded that he had not. At the question of whether he had visited her for other reasons more often than for confession, he answered that he had. When asked to elaborate the reasons for this, he answered it was "for the various celebrations and feasts that the nuns take part in, for spiritual guidance outside of confession, because of the long-standing friendship held by their families, for whom they serve as messengers, and for matters of scientific interest."

When asked what he meant by the latter, he said that Sister Ágata had developed a taste for studying in her free time from her obligations to her convent, to her sisters, and to God, of course, and that she had asked him for advice for developing the machine, whose function was very well discerned by Brother Severino. When asked if he knew the purpose of said machine, he said he knew no more than that it was related to a series of experiments that would augment her knowledge of acoustics, which he admired, since "what talents God gives and are not used are talents given to the Devil."

At the question of what his help in constructing this machine consisted of, he answered that it was "in the mathematic calculation of certain elements of the machine, the discussion of certain principles of acoustics, and little more."

When asked about the accusations made by Sister María Devota del Niño Jesús of seduction and witchcraft, he declares these are products of mental confusion on the part of "poor Sister María." He would like to make very clear in this report that Sister María is victim to various illnesses, as she has made apparent since joining the convent, which give her sudden increases of humors in the brain, provoking delusions like those of a fever which, far from making her a mystic, daze and confuse her greatly.

Her confessor has taken advantage of this condition to create a series of lies damaging to the faith, such as that Sister María has the gift of prophecy and visions of the future, stories that he himself writes, exalting the scrambled imagination of Sister María during her confession, then sells to those who will buy them. As he does this without her knowledge, granting none of the earnings to the sister and encouraging her fantasies for his own benefit, it is evident that Sister María is a victim of her own confessor, an extremely delicate role which some unscrupulous men force on some poor women. Perhaps the words of Sister María regarding her relationship with Sister Ágata de la Luz were a cry for attention toward her own confessor and the harm he inflicts upon her.

God forbid that seduction be added to the list of these wicked acts, as all know that solicitation from priests to faithful women during their confessions is a very common crime, despite being punished so horrifically by the Tribunal of the Holy Office. May God bless Sister María Devota and ensure her wellbeing, and may this Holy Process do her justice.

Statement of Sister María Devota del Niño Jesús, mystic

Sister María Devota, in the world outside named Delfina Figueroa, states herself to be from Cholula, Puebla, and to have cloistered herself two years ago with the black veil, that is to say, devoted solely to prayer, after her relatives requested the favor of her admission, as this convent of Corpus Christi had never accepted a novice that was not descended from indigenous nobility. She insisted on this convent, however, because she had seen it in one of her visions while in Puebla. It is urgent that she make her statement, says she, in order to dethrone all the lies that the nuns and servants have told in this Holy Process, so that she be allowed to relate the events which she wanted to recount before the interrogation.

Sister María declares having noticed, since her arrival at the convent, illicit relations between Brother Alfonso de Alba and Sister Ágata de la Luz because her cell is adjacent to Sister Ágata's and this proximity allowed her to hear, on multiple nights, sounds "typical of fornication" and laughter at late hours of the night while the rest of the convent slept. She does not rule out that in these meetings they both were invoking a demon, hearing them so disinclined toward repentance for their actions. This repeated conduct has affected her opinion, not only because of the exposure to such a lack of decorum, but because in recent days both of them began the wicked project of making the machine which is presented to the Holy Office as evidence of her conduct against Christianity.

For this purpose, Sister Ágata asked Brother Alfonso to extract forbidden books from the libraries to which he had access, and though she claimed to be unable to remember their titles, she did remember the names "Copernicus, Eustachi, Isako (or Isaías) Newtonono, Aristotle, Vansalva," among various others which she did not remember. She knows this because she saw the books one hot day when the nun was working with her door half open.

With the complicity of Sister Elena, the gatekeeper of the convent, Sister Ágata had many encounters in the visiting room with Brother Alfonso, under the pretext of her confession. Though she supposes that certain solicitations were the purposes of those encounters, she remembers that often the two spoke in hushed tones with other Indian sisters, as if conspiring against who knows whom. She confesses that she even thought of writing letters to the benefactors of the convent with the goal of begging them to admit more creoles immediately, because it is known that the Indians are resentful and envious and could be planning to harm her, for being the minority.

This filled her with fear, until one day, she had a vision: she was setting off to drink her evening hot chocolate when the divine Baby Jesus appeared to her. His golden curls and luxurious robes gleamed at the end of the hallway. With His little hand, He signaled for her to retrace her steps. The door of Sister Ágata's bedchamber was open, the Baby Jesus entered through it, and she told herself that if her infant husband was doing so, surely there was nothing to fear from it.

The baby Jesus directed her to Sister Ágata's bed, the form of which called her attention: it was like a platform with a mattress atop and looked more elevated than was normal. Searching with the help of the Divine Child, she found a mechanism that opened an ingenious little door, and there it was revealed that the base of the bed was hollow, which allowed one to store all sorts of things. It was there that Sister Ágata kept the artifact and the forbidden books.

Then the young Jesus showed her to the large wardrobe, and He told her that both of them would hide there until dawn. When Sister Ágata returned, Sister María could hear in detail the illicit relations between Brother Alfonso de Alba and the sister, concerning the manufacturing of the apparatus and its diabolical purpose. Sister María Devota feared the reaction of the Divine Child Jesus in response to the couple's touching and kissing, but in His infinite wisdom and modesty, His Majesty disappeared during these dealings.

Sister Ágata and Brother Alfonso, after their pleasure, abandoned themselves to the reading of books and based on what one of them said, decided that they needed a piece of skin like that on a drum, but thinner, for the artifact to work. Sister Ágata said that they should hurry to build it, since she did not know "how much longer she could meet with her," she said, which Sister María did not immediately understand.

Brother Alfonso said that such a situation was extraordinary and that they should take advantage as much as possible of this window that had opened, he said, "between their two times." Sister Ágata said to Brother Alfonso that it was precisely for this reason that she had made a list of questions for her to respond to in the next communication, which would take place on Wednesday at six o'clock in the evening because dusk was the only time and the well the only place that allowed the encounter. Sister María asked the child Jesus to help her memorize what her sister said next in order to relate it to the Holy Office. Sister Ágata read from her list the following:

—Once the sounds, that is, the messages, were *recorded* and sent to all persons selected for the revolt, how could these people listen to it? Sister Ágata said she thought it necessary to construct another machine. And how could this machine be brought to so many people in the cities and in the country when she was in the cloister?

—Whether these *recorded* voices could be made to project louder. Whether it was possible to apply to a small artifact the principles of architecture which enhance sound. Whether a wooden box or a sea shell would be useful for this enterprise.

—Whether any of these languages that she has *recorded* with her sisters survives: Nahuatl, Maya, Otomi, Purépecha, Zapoteca, Mixteca. Or if none have survived, which would mean that neither she nor her sisters were successful.

—What the future is like in other aspects, whether people like her and her sisters enjoy liberty and happiness. And if it is not against God's will for her to have this knowledge.

Sister Ágata, narrated Sister María, told Brother Alfonso that the next day, at the time at which it was possible to have the encounter, she would go to the underground well to speak with and listen to the woman. Brother Alfonso promised that the next day he would order the skin needed for the machine from a craftsman, who also makes drums on Donceles Street, named Ignacio.

"If you doubt my testimony, go and ask him," assured Sister María.

She finished her speech by saying that she would never forget the terrors of that night, when she discovered one of her sisters engaged in carnality and the supposed agreement with a woman, who Sister Ágata believes lives in another time, but who is not another woman but the Devil tricking her into constructing an artifact to begin a revolt among the Indian people, who, cunning and bitter as they are, will see themselves compelled by him to commit cruelties against Spaniards and creoles, forced to adore his horrendous idols, which had already been defeated by the power of Christ.

Sister María says that she sees this in the repeated visions that her gift of mysticism allows her to anticipate, that, as a spokesperson of the One True God, the Holy Office should not let her testimony fall on deaf ears, and that for the time being she hopes Brother Alfonso and Sister Ágata will be punished with the green candle carried by heretics and death by fire. And that, despite all the suffering they have caused her, it is clear that she wishes for the salvation of both souls through repentance. Having said this, she fainted and could no longer be questioned for the time being.

Statement of Sister Ágata

Sister Ágata de la Luz, named in the outside world Aurora Ruiz, is from Mexico City. She cloistered herself seven years ago, being the daughter in her family chosen by God. She wears a white veil, for which she carries out various corporal tasks in addition to praying for the souls of the faithful. She pleads innocent of the accusations that Sister María Devota has made against her, "though not all of them," she concedes, which put the Tribunal on alert. They began the interrogation immediately. Which crimes does she then plead guilty to, of the following: bewitchment, delusion, bigamy (having engaged in carnal behavior with a man while the bride of Christ), or heresy? To which Sister Ágata responded that she was guilty of none of these charges, only of certain behaviors expressed by poor Sister María Devota, whom the humors referred to by Fray Alfonso have left, indeed, very confused.

Sister Ágata admits to having read, yes, "some forbidden books, but none in their entirety." She read copies censored by the Holy Office, of course, approved and facilitated by her confessor, who is most interested in the salvation of her soul. He sees her interest in physics and mathematics as edifying, as long as she puts this knowledge toward service to the community, which is just what she wishes to do with the artifact. She asks the scribe to register her words as accurately as possible.

When asked if she has had carnal encounters with her confessor, or if he had made solicitations in the confession booth or any other space of the cloister, Sister Ágata responded no. At the question of what the purpose of the artifact constructed in her cell was, Sister Ágata responded that "it's a *recorder* of sounds, a machine capable of fixing your words in the air; just as words and drawings can stay written using a chisel on stone, wood, or metal, sound can be kept in some base material, in order to later be duplicated and propagated far from its place of origin, like books."

The Tribunal, a bit perplexed, asked if the idea had been inspired by the woman from the future whom Sister María had heard mentioned, to which Sister Ágata responded that "Sister

María confuses intention with inspiration, because I started thinking of these things after the death of my grandmother, who hardly had anyone to speak her language with, so she never taught it to me. My intention in constructing the machine was to provide, to the people in the time to come, love, knowledge, the languages of our present, of people like the grandmothers of all the nuns in the convent," she said. "And the love of God, of course," she added.

The officials asked if her intention was to begin an Indian revolt, and she appeared distressed at this idea. She said, "God knows that my intentions were good." At the question of whether she achieved her mission using common resources behind the backs of the prioress and Church authorities, she responded: "Unfortunately, I failed. The apparatus does not work as it should."

At this time the Tribunal asked Brother Severino to perform one of the planned tests of the functionality of the machine. Brother Severino explained to the Holy Office that he would perform the test using a plate of Tepezcohuite tree soap to see if it were possible to record the sounds suspended in the air "like words in stone." Sister Ágata was asked to assist him in the preparation of the artifact and, in general, in such an experiment.

Then the nun asked the father to speak clearly into the cone, reciting some verses or singing some song without pausing. Brother Severino began reciting the Ave María, but the Tribunal reprimanded him for speaking the name of the Virgin in vain, so after a bit of thought he began to recite some verses from Brother Luis de León. Sister Ágata moved the handle energetically, which caused the disc of soap to spin, the thick needle leaving a circular mark on the surface. The skin attached to the embroidery frame fluctuated with every breath taken by Brother Severino. At every movement of this membrane, the brass plate holding the needle made it move subtly, altering the mark on the soap. When the father finished, Sister Ágata stopped moving the handle.

On the plate of soap was a spiral mark with subtle variations on the surface. In this moment, a brief feeling of achievement and joy was experienced. Brother Severino then said that the accused had lied: the machine did work, and the sound had been written in the soap. To which Sister Ágata responded: "But you can't hear it."

At the question of whether the voices of her sisters that Sister María heard the night that Juana reported her to the prioress were the result of this experience of the artifact, she responded that they were. At the question of where she had kept this and other soap discs where she made such *recordings*, Sister Ágata answered that, when they turned out imperfectly, she boiled and remolded them "to reuse the expensive material in subsequent trials," since she had taken, as all the nuns had, a vow of poverty.

At the question of whether these were the matters that Sister María Devota had heard from her that night when she supposedly had shared her bed with Brother Alfonso, the accused responded that these were the matters that she sometimes pondered out loud in the solitude of her cell, and which Sister María "surely, in her wild imagination, transformed into the scene which she narrated to the Tribunal, entirely fictitious."

Given the known character of Sister María Devota, of whom none of her sisters had testified in favor (the opposite of Sister Ágata), the trial came to an uncertain silence. Sister Ágata, arrogating her own defense, humbly asked permission to propose the following to the Holy Office, in order to eliminate the suspicion against her, her confessor, and the innocent sisters of the convent: to entomb the machine in a resilient box with a strong lock in a location where nobody could reach it, along with the soap disc and other objects that show evidence of the time (a portrait or altarpiece, some praise to the ecclesial authorities, a missive explaining what is kept there) until somebody more fitting than a nun was able to create an artifact that would revive them in the future, "let's say, in some two hundred and fifty years, or however long Your Reverences deem prudent."

The Tribunal was satisfied with this idea, which would accompany an admonitory punishment for Sister Ágata de la Luz and Brother Alfonso de Alba, of course. Then a party would be thrown with fireworks, where the wine and sweets and cooked snacks of Sister Rosa would flow. Why not bury this treasure in the underground well of the convent? It would have to be on a Wednesday at six o'clock in the evening. It could be this very Wednesday, in fact, assured the provisor of the convent, as there would surely be enough food for the celebration.

At this time Sister María Devota del Niño Jesús began thrashing on the floor in violent spasms, uttering insults toward Sister Ágata, her sisters, and the Tribunal. "It's an ambush!" she shouted. "Don't go to the well! She and the people from the future will come through the window to destroy us!"

The officials took her to a secure location to perform an exorcism, God protect her soul.

The Tribunal of the Holy Inquisition declares Sister Ágata de la Luz innocent of the charges of delusion, bewitchment, bigamy, and heresy, carrying a warning and minor penitence, and sets a positive precedence for the trial of Fray Alfonso de Alba, which will take place on Wednesday of the coming week, prior to the celebration of the burying of the artifact at six o'clock in the evening in the underground well of the Convent for Noble Indians of Corpus Christi, Mexico, year of our Lord 1779.

THE ART OF MEMORY

When the vast cloud of dust settled on the ground, light and silky as if time itself had finally arrived to its destination, Cordelia woke up. The platform's shield had held up despite everything, and the blow to her head was apparently not too severe. She dreamt of water, lots of water, and rays of sun filtering through the thicket in a forest she had never seen before.

Coming back to reality, Cordelia realized that everyone was dead. The control room was a tangle of sheet metal, flesh, and blood. The static signals from the radio and television took no notice of the state of the world, whether people were holding their breath or resignedly preparing for the end, or whether the wailing and gnashing of teeth had already begun, as foretold by religions that predicted Judgement Day with seven-headed dragons wearing crowns of precious stones like Cordelia had imagined since the nuns taught her about it in school.

How much longer until the end of everything? She didn't remember what they had said (Cordelia, among many other things, had a bad memory). The launch failing, and this catastrophe happening, had been suggested as an extremely remote possibility.

The hope of lifting off with unprecedented force, of searching for our *brothers* (as they proclaimed themselves), of finding them and getting—at last!—all the answers, had the whole world intoxicated with joy.

The message had been brief, almost affectionate: Come, let's talk about how our world and yours have grown without anybody's help. We are not alone in the universe. We are orphans and brothers. At least that's what Cordelia's careful translation had revealed.

The orders were meticulous, precise, obvious to the point of exasperation. How had they never imagined this type of travel before? It was as simple as tossing a bottle into the sea, a bottle that would travel the universe on waves of pure energy. It was hard to understand that the chaotic journey would, against all odds, have a plan, a predetermined destination. The key was not to design a route, said the brothers, but a *landscape*. That is, it was up to humans to create a tide of energy sufficient to push their bottle far enough to crash onto the other shore in a short amount of time. The brothers would be there, waiting for three cosmonauts.

It could go badly, said many, a trivial error could end it all. The energy of the launch was programmed to behave like a wave that could only ebb if it was channeled into the trajectory of the bottle. On the other hand, if it failed, it would come back again and again, again and again until it eroded the Earth to dust like water turns rocks to sand. But even those who foresaw the worst-case scenarios believed the risk was worth it. The launch pad was built, the ship was designed (it was the press's fault that the "bottle" could never be called anything else) and a team was formed, a chosen few who would reach the brothers and respond to the message. Cordelia was not among them. The training required to withstand the journey was never-ending, and she didn't pass the tests, never thought she could. But they couldn't leave her out. She had translated the message, she understood the brothers' thoughts more than anyone else, and if that weren't enough, she was the one who had planned the expedition. That's why she would be on the platform, the safest place to be because of its distance from the bottle, doing nothing but observing the launch. She knew this was little more than a symbolic gesture. The ones who didn't make mistakes would be in the control room, the ones who would take home the trophies when our form of life arrived safely.

And now this version of life, the human one, was about to end.

Cordelia sobbed, wanted to cry because of the failure, the death of all those people, but for now she had to power through and think. Was it one hour and 45 minutes before the next wave?

What a disaster, Cordelia. She could never remember anything, not even in these circumstances. This is why you couldn't be a cosmonaut, she told herself. That's where it must have started: could the crew still be alive? Maybe the protection of the platform extended to them as well. It would be miraculous.

Cordelia's imagination worked prodigiously. She assumed they were alive, a bit shaken, but stable. She could try to launch them in the next wave, and they could still make the meeting. There wasn't much left to lose, and if it worked ...

Then it wasn't over yet. This version of life would continue somewhere else.

She ran to the bottle, which looked intact. It was still the perfect structure to carry them to that unfamiliar dock. She imagined space, the roundness of the planets that the cosmonauts would see in passing, the colors of the nebulas, the hoarse beating of the pulsars ... she ignored the motionless bundles of hair, fabric, and teeth that she glimpsed here and there. She ignored the pain of remembering them, alive and enthusiastic just a few hours before.

She manipulated the controls to open the bottle, her fingers trembling over the flow of glass panels on the console. She was out of breath. She blamed that on her thick thighs, her habitual clumsiness. This is why you could never be a cosmonaut.

As she entered the bottle, she didn't call out to anyone. She wanted to avoid the moment when nobody would respond. Deep down she knew: their bodies were frozen in their final gestures, but they weren't expressions of pain (they might be, maybe, of surprise). Death made their skin glow with that strange, beautiful splendor. She couldn't help but feel lucky not to have been chosen. Right away she regretted thinking it. She was a horrible person. She was not a cosmonaut (her memory, the failed calculations, her body weight, emotional instability, and, oh, so many other flaws), but she had planned out the questions, what that first ever exchange would be like, how we would tell them what we were. Did that redeem her in some way? What a stupid pretension, she thought.

How much longer until death?

Outside, some distance away on the launchpad's lookout station, she saw threadbare national flags still waving in the air. The bleachers were empty, abandoned in fear. What happened to those people?

The alarm system rang. Well, something had to keep working after all this. It announced the next wave: 25 *minutes.*

Would the rest of the planet suffer? Would they be in pain?

The risk committee had concluded that they wouldn't, but they'd also said the launch would be a success. She couldn't be certain of anything.

Why was she still alive? She, the clumsiest and stupidest and meanest and never a cosmonaut.

And what if she pushed the bottle into the second wave?

19 minutes.

All of her mistakes had been solvable. They would have chosen her if she had stuck to the diet, if she had double-checked the results of her calculations, if she had figured out a way to not get distracted, to remember the important stuff ...

There was one. The art of memory. Simonides of Ceos' mnemonic device, that she remembered very well; such useless things one keeps in one's head.

It was a wonderful formula: you went to a place, for example, the façade of an old church, and you assigned every architectural element to one part of your memory. Let's say you wanted to keep in the memory of the last time you saw your mother. The alcove could be her eyes. The columns, her dress. The door, her words. Every element keeps a piece of the idea, of the moment. And when you've put each one of them in this place, and after a while you return to it, the façade will orchestrate the memory for you.

10 minutes.

What room, what architecture could there be up there to keep what we were? On second thought, the unknown expanse of space was the perfect place for an altar to human memory. So vain, so contradictory. So ephemeral.

6 minutes.

Maybe there really wasn't much worth preserving. What significance would an almanac of dates and boring landscapes have for the others? And even then, would our tiny beauties mean anything?

The response message approved by the assembly remained as limited and hypocritical as when they prohibited nudity from the gold disc on the Voyagers.

She would describe nude bodies, first the joy of discovering one's own, and others second. The feeling of another hand fitting into ours. The temperature of the belly, always warm, busy, and noisy. The bodies of children, drawn in a single stroke, running to the shower. She would keep them in a pink nebula ... NGC 6357, the most beautiful of the dim nebulae, a nursery for baby stars.

5 minutes.

The smell of trees. The nighttime whispering of a forest. Sh2-277 in Orion could be a good place for the branches, the freshness, the dew. The hoot of an owl and the roar of a bear.

4 minutes.

A rainbow in a puddle of oil spilled on concrete. Dancing, apple liqueur. The smell of corn. The phantom rainbow that appears for only one person when they're in front of a waterfall, that they'll lose if they move, and that nobody else can see, ever. Clouds in shades of orange and violet. Ghosts and the sorrows of haunted houses. She'll need an empty asteroid to store them in, the shell of a celestial body.

3 minutes.

She's decided that the cosmonauts will have the best funeral rites in space. The red dwarves will be perennial flowers over their graves. They will never wither.

She found in the cabinet, among other things, photographs of the crew's families, a change of suits and, curiously, a packet of *Myosotis Sylvatica* seeds, that little blue flower whose petals look like mouse ears: the forget-me-not. The suit is tight, but the oxygen is flowing and she can move in it. And what did it matter if the planet likely wouldn't be around after the wave and neither would she or the suit except as dust? Or not even that.

2 minutes.

She had taken on the role of an impostor. What will the brothers say, if she even gets to see them, when they see her arrive with three bodies, a suit that's too tight and a packet of forget-me-nots? She would have loved to bring aboard the loyalty of a dog and the harmony of a cat. But there were entire nebulae for that. She'll look for the Cat's

Eye to preserve purring and fill Sirius with the memory of dogs who bark at the sea.

The desert. Reptiles.

It's very likely the wave won't push the bottle. But if there was one thing to be said about humans, it was that they kept trying until the very end. At least the best of us did, thought Cordelia.

1 minute.

Ah, the rain wetting the earth, kisses on cold lips, the smell of carrion. Music. Birds in flight, fire. A movie theatre audience left speechless at the end of a sad story. Velvet. Fish. Spiderwebs. A father feeding his daughter in tiny spoonfuls.

Cordelia sees that the wave is near and lets the bottle fall into the empty space that approaches.

In the wave, her eyes catch a glimpse of the merciful face of time.

THE BRIDGE

I've dreamt of her every day for a month. Someone else might find it frightening, but it was comforting to me, until last night. I was always very close to my aunt, and her death was bitterly nostalgic for me. I look in the mirror and see her nose in mine; I recognize her long nails in the pink half-moon of my hands; I know that if I live long enough to get old, my body will be a reflection of hers. Flesh and blood don't lie. They betray our belonging to that liquid group called a family, forever pulling us into its tide.

I'm only now paying close attention to my dreams because I don't have my usual distractions and escape routes at hand; the lights are out. Even though it's barely dusk, the house has already gotten dark. I was watching TV when the blackout hit. I try turning it on once, twice, three times in fewer than five minutes, knowing it's useless but resisting my thoughts, resisting being alone with myself and what's bothering me. Reality filters through the kitchen window. The flight of a pair of doves, the crash of dishes being washed, neighbors wandering around the electric meters, guessing at the cause of the blackout.

I surrender to the lazy train of my thoughts, lie down in bed to wait for her return. Then I remember the atmosphere, the light, the taste of the dream.

***

I'm outside in the sun. The treetops are tall and green. The grass beneath my feet is tall and whispers with the passing of fresh, almost cold wind, feeling like it does at the beginning of spring. My grandparents' house, where my aunt lived her entire life, is ahead of me across a churning river that shimmers in the daylight and bubbles white foam over rocks. I approach the shore and confirm that I can't cross it, the stream's topaz color attesting to its treacherous depth. The wrought iron door, whose twisted bars end in golden points, is closed. Behind the gate my aunt watches me. She has the same hairstyle that she has in photos where I'm just a baby, the same scandalous makeup à go-go with false lashes that made her eyes pop, the same frozen smile from the pictures. I know she's dead.

I still want to cross.

My aunt puts a hand through the bars. With the other she tries to open the door.

"Wait! Don't fall. I'll go to you, don't come over!" she shouts to me with that jovial voice I remember so well.

I'm glad to hear her, to see her again. I see her leave the door of the house half open. I know that inside there are more people, all dead, all mine.

But I'm not scared.

The river stands between us.

The neighbors have assembled. I can hear them yell, organize, go up and down stairs. I guess the light won't be back anytime soon. The noise doesn't stop me from feeling drowsy. The soft amber darkness marks the contours of the dresser, the lamp, the pictures. I drift off, but I don't close my eyes; I don't want to fall asleep. After last night, I don't want to dream of her again.

***

"Don't move. I'll come to you. Bring something we can use," she said every night.

It took me a while to understand the necessity of building a bridge. In the dream scenario, the extensive riverbank continues into the horizon, and at its end I sense the abyss of a waterfall. On the other side, the water rushes down tiered stones that get lost in the green blackness of the forest. It made sense to look for logs to build the structure; but dream logic is something else. I went into the forest and found random materials, objects that came my way: a dress with gemstone appliques, the bar of a sliding door, a plastic salt-shaker in the shape of a tomato ...

While I hunted, I was a child wearing winter clothes. I realized these trinkets were pieces of time, a familiar time that we both had shared. Insignificant memories buried in my mind that had been the props of my childhood, of her youth, and that now regained all of their relevance.

These relics of my own archeology became so precious to me!

When I had gathered as many things as I could carry, I brought them to the river and dropped them on the surface with the care that one takes with fragile paper boats. My aunt was glad, and so was I. The majority of the objects floated, traveling fast to the other shore, but others sank, which made me very sad. My aunt rearranged them like a puzzle. Then she put one of her bare feet on top and pressed down to test their strength. From the opposite shore she smiled, encouraged me, using the same words she used after my recitals or when I passed a hard test in school.

I was so pleased, in the end, to find these treasures that I couldn't wait for the next night to discover what else the forest would give us.

In the dreams there was no trace of the final, devastating image that I had of my aunt. Naked on a soaking wet towel, mascara running down her cheeks, mouth open in a last attempt to inhale. Hands and feet twisted like branches. Hair standing on end, the only ghost of the electric charge that went in through her feet and exploded in her chest.

On the curtain I see a shadow of birds flying erratically. The neighbors listen to a message I can't decipher through a beat-up laptop. Should I go out and join them? I have no desire to move. They start up their cars. The voices rise in pitch. "Why risk it?!" shouts one. And I think the same thing. I sink into the mattress like it's quicksand. I see no reason to get up, to try turning on the television one more time. My body seems to be convincing itself of this. It's as if I've made myself ill with apathy since the bad dream.

Before last night the atmosphere of the dream was soothing joy. My aunt progressed with the construction of the bridge, impressive to see. Composed of so many miniatures and curious textures and unique fragments, it stood between the two of us, more tangible than anything we had shared in real life.

Until my excursions to the forest became useless.

I found many more objects, but they sank to the bottom of the river when I tried to use them for building. They didn't pass who knows what test. Maybe it was that the pincushion, the little soaps wrapped up in tissue paper, the silver tray were tied, for me, in my memory, more to my grandmother than to her. The bridge was almost complete, but she still couldn't cross. Every night of the past week I dug and dug into the earth with mediocre results. The appearance of my aunt changed: from the other shore I could see her exhaustion, her sorrow.

That's how I found half the objects that were left: the sad ones.

I found her wedding album, some photographs peeling away from the self-adhering plastic. I found dirty baby clothes stacked on a mattress covered with worn sheets; a couple of her antique dolls that always scared me, their grimy plastic faces smiling from inside plush animal bodies. All the letters she never opened, yellowing papers, unpaid bills, advertisements, sprouting from the dirt like withered flowers in silent reproach. Suddenly, I grew up: in the dream I was an adult looking for the belongings that were dearest to my aunt, who was already crippled by melancholy. I picked the things up and brought them to the river with a happy face so that she'd know these unpleasant memories didn't undermine my love for her. I wanted her to look at me, to feel my affection; I wanted to eliminate the guilt I felt for not having always been there and at the same time, give her some kind of consolation. With almost hungry movements I lay the rest of the objects in the river, a ravenous sapphire tongue of memorabilia that gave off dazzling sparks when the final stretch of the bridge was complete. My aunt's face, inflamed, dead, swollen from the water, stared at me expressionless from the opposite shore.

And I woke up.

Night has fallen. Outside, silence.

I don't hear anything until a scream explodes against the windows of the building across from mine. I try to move, but I can't. I think I'm suspended in the horrible state of sleeping with my eyes open. I try to wake up, but no, I'm not asleep. The shouts keep happening in the apartments on my street, surging and bursting like soap bubbles. There's a constant noise, the sound of *something* dragging itself. Something sliding up the stairs and still ascending, another something slithering down the street, something else lurching on the floor above me. Far away, muffled, I can just hear a sound like the cries of a gravely wounded person.

Soon there are hundreds.

I can't move. I fall without falling in infinite repetition. I feel like I'm sinking into the mire of the dream and floating to the surface only to sink again. I'm condemned to lie on my side with my head facing the front door. I can't even close my eyes to avoid seeing what comes through it.

There's a cloying, acid scent in the air.

I hear the scratches of someone begging to enter my house. She doesn't have enough strength to tear down the door, but as the minutes pass, it's clear she does have the persistence necessary not to leave. I hear her long breaths, the clicking of a tongue perhaps too short to articulate what it wants to say.

But I hear her in my head: "Don't move. I'll come to you."

Outside, the screams multiply as quickly as the moans. I somehow understand that each thing dragging itself is looking for its feeble prey, immobile as I am. The venom inoculated in our dreams effectively paralyzes.

The television suddenly switches on, the screen painfully illuminating the comforter, the lamp, the pictures, the entrance. The light has come back, and it brings no hope with it.

I can see how the door opens. The nude body of my aunt crosses the threshold, her poor blue-green skin resounding with each step, eyeliner smeared over the greyish skin of her eyelids, mouth and tongue purple, hands extended forward, searching.

When her eyes find me, I know she's not there in that body covered in maggots. An alien terror has animated my aunt's body. I feel it leaning like an invalid on the solid walls of her memory, that labyrinth of entrails; I feel how it grows with the vibrant connections it finds inside of her. How it's strengthened by *our* connection.

Because it was me, it was us, the ones who once loved them, who built the bridge that brought them to our flesh and blood. All the people screaming outside have woven their own shrouds.

Pulled forever into the tide of love. Ah, family.

I see the hunger in what were my aunt's lips, which half-open softly. The terror shows me her gums, shining and vile like pale emeralds.

As her teeth sink into my arm, the venom allows me one movement: my mouth opens to scream, and the cry is like another bridge that allows me to cross the river.

The door of my grandparents' house opens slowly, a resigned welcome.

THE SYNCHRONY OF TOUCH

We loved each other, but not how Neruda and the telenovelas said we would. We had dated, and we had failed. When he discovered that my favorite extracurricular activity was breaking the hearts of professors on the faculty, he got revenge by coming to a party on another girl's arm, and I decided to fade away from his life. Everything would have ended there. But we resisted living in a world without each other. The phone still rang every night at the same time as always until, months later, I answered. We apologized. The relief we felt was instantaneous. We started chatting about whatever bullshit we could think of; it was impossible for us to discover a new song, movie, or book without urgently telling the other about it. We talked for hours, trying to catch Meaning, that elusive creature that sometimes allowed itself to be seen, by the tail. We longed to find the key to who knows what. We assumed we would find it while talking.

One afternoon, when I was about to go to the supermarket with my mom, he called. His voice sounded distant and metallic; he was speaking from a public phone. He was so excited that even my mother heard his yelling from the receiver. She sensed this would take time and she'd better leave me alone.

"I found something. Something amazing."

"What?"

"A flower."

"A flower," I said, just to let him know I had heard him.

"You have no idea what it does. You need to come over, but like, now, right now."

He had tried all the drugs; I, more curious about sex than stimulants back then, had only accompanied him in his pilgrimage through each of them.

"Where are you?"

"In San Agustín del Mar." I laughed out loud. He was more than three hundred miles from the city.

"Get out of there, dummy. When are you coming back?"

"I'm serious. Come. I saved you some blackberries."

"I can't. I have to finish my thesis, remember?"

"You will, believe me. I saw you finishing it, but you need to see the flower. I don't know how to explain it."

I suddenly got scared that his brain was completely fried. What if he was on a bad trip? What if his call was a product of delirium or paranoia induced by who knows what chemical cocktail? Was I going to have to talk to his mom? His mom scared me.

"Tell me something," I said, to get a feel for his usual equilibrium of sanity/insanity. "Are you in danger of becoming a surfer, eating flowers and never coming back? Do you need me to come get you?"

"Calm down, I'm fine. But you have to come. This is important. And I need you to help me understand this, and not just because you're a biologist." His tone indicated that it wasn't a real emergency, and yet …

"An almost-biologist, and a pretty bad one," I reminded him, because I hadn't been out in the field for quite a while.

Between our voices came the interference of the recording of the ghostly operator, indicating that the call time was almost over. I didn't say anything more, but he knew that I never ignored calls for help, always trying to *understand* whatever the problem was. That was my addiction.

"Time's up! I'm in the cabins on the summit. Be careful."

We were spoiled kids, but it wouldn't be a lie to say there was some emptiness inside us, fertile and ready to host a seed. We lived with our parents in that intermediate phase between degree and unemployment, beyond lucky, and any money we got our hands on we could use to satisfy our vices: bootleg DVDs burned by street cinephiles, albums, concerts, parties, or books. Taking advantage of our reputation as good students, we wasted time; we escaped into our music all afternoon instead of doing our homework, staring at the ceiling, or we searched the internet (when nobody else was using the telephone line) to learn how to lucid dream in obscure chat rooms on Yahoo!

Anyway: we reached out our hands and took for granted that our random whims would be granted, like impromptu travel. It wasn't a ridiculous request: many universities did "revolutionary tourism" with the ingenious idea of *helping the indigenous peoples*, so for them it was a blessing that we were self-absorbed cowards. Spending the night in cabins in the mountains and not participating in the Zapatista revolution calmed them down, but only because when they were young, they weren't hippie enough to know that the only reason to go to San Agustín del Mar was psychotropic tourism. My process of persuasion included unrealistic promises.

"I'll come back and get my degree right away, I promise."

"It's not about that—it hasn't even been a month since you got out of the hospital."

"But I'm fine now! I'll take care of myself."

"The last time you said that you were collecting samples in the rain all night. Don't make me remind you how many days you were hospitalized."

The overprotectiveness, though understandable, crushed me like a ton of bricks. I got permission with the condition that I would never leave without my medicine and that Claudia, the vertex of the scalene triangle that formed the three of us, would accompany me.

"If she's not going, forget it. She'll balance the two of you out. She deserves a vacation because she already graduated. But above all, she won't let you get distracted," my mom said, rubbing salt in the wound.

The first four hours of the trip were full of gossip and laughter, but the last three to San Agustín del Mar I got more carsick than I've ever been in my life, maybe a foreshadowing of the vertigo that was to come. The rusted truck, which we shared with chickens, bales of hay, and crates of merchandise, ascended on a spiral road. Sucking on a lemon didn't help, and I didn't even feel capable of putting new batteries in the CD player to distract myself with music. I cuddled up to Claudia and closed my eyes, trying to stop the nausea. When we arrived, the clean, cold air and the view, a sea of clouds kissing the tops of a forest of pine trees, soothed me.

We found the cabins right away, but Ekar wasn't there. From the clues we exchanged with Epifanía, the owner of the place, we learned that he was indeed staying there and that he had gone on an excursion with Toribio, her husband, to look for the *water children*. Claudia and I turned onto the town's main street, ate non-magic mushroom soup, quesadillas, hot chocolate, and pan de yema. The ladies in the dining room praised our appetites and warned us that we may have eaten too much if we were planning on *traveling* later. We walked through the forest before the sun set. At this altitude, they told us, there was fog, but if we went down, following the silver trail of the river, the climate would change to almost tropical. Like a promise of the sea, the hot earth there was already sprouting bananas and coffee beans.

"How are you?" Claudia was worried my lungs wouldn't withstand the cold humidity of the fog and the walk.

"Splendid." I lied at times, saying that everything was okay, and suddenly it wasn't a lie: little by little I started to feel I was breathing like never before and that I kept in my chest the scent of oak (*Quercus rugosa*), the shine of pine resin (*Pinaceae*), and its needles that just scraped the view of the bed of clouds at our feet. A crazy idea crossed my mind: maybe I had died in the hospital and this, us two being in this scene, was heaven.

Ekar was skinnier, but euphoric as always. His long eyelashes projected a shadow on his dark circles. When we found each other, we hurtled toward one another like a pack of animals. Dusk fell. The burning sky framed our silhouettes against the light in a window pane. I took a picture of our reflection with the camera that I never learned to use in my entire degree and that, of course (I told myself), I would handle with extreme care. But every action was of good intent. None of what we actually experienced in those days could have been captured in a static, two-dimensional image, outside of time and touch.

Ekar had us follow him to the house's kitchen. On Epifanía and Toribio's table lay the harvest of mushrooms. The *water children*. I recognized the mythical *Psilocybe mexicana* that I had seen so often in books, but I had never imagined the true intensity of the bluish-black color that coagulated in them like an otherworldly blood clot. There were many, wet and dark, of different shapes and sizes. Toribio explained to us the difference between the varieties: the Golden Teachers and Landslides, Pajaritos and San Isidros; he told us how the rain and fallen leaves or horse and cow droppings cultivate their predictable but strange birth. He asked if we already knew how to take them, what we would feel, how long it would last, et cetera. He mentioned that neither he nor Epifanía officiated rituals.

They simply gathered the mushrooms and offered lodging to those who wanted to eat them.

"Is it all right if she has asthma?" asked Claudia.

Toribio said that it would even cure me. Epifanía started to make me a tea that promised the same. Then he continued.

"This really should be done properly with someone who knows. I know how to tell them apart, I know how many to eat and how many not to, but that's not *knowing*. You need someone to guide your soul. That's the important part, and nobody values it anymore."

"The ones that offer you a sweat lodge package with an exfoliant and a mushroom trip don't understand anything. Those are shit. I understand them, but fuck it, that's not wisdom. All the same: I don't know anything about anything either. Come on, I'll give you a sweater. Don't freeze on us," said Epifanía, and I followed her.

Meanwhile, Ekar helped arrange on hoja santa leaves the different doses that the hosts would bring to their guests: eight pajaritos, three landslides, and two San Isidros for the group in Cabin 6; mushroom tea, the mildest way to consume them, for posh Cabin 4, et cetera.

"And watch out for the pigs," warned Toribio. He wasn't talking about farm animals.

"If anyone tries to scare you, tell them that it's not illegal to do this here, that we govern ourselves by usos y costumbres. Be careful," Epifanía chided when we returned to the kitchen, and she offered us a dinner of tamales. Claudia and I accepted, of course, guessing that we'd have a long night ahead of us.

But it wasn't. The chorus of trees sang noisily. We sat on the little porch. I marveled at the number of stars we could see: white flares interrupted from time to time by the tousled conifers. Ekar took the blankets off the beds and covered us with them. Then he put something in my hand that, in the moonlight, looked like a tiny person. It was the flower. Its petals had oxidized. I could tell it had been cut several hours ago. Even so, I noted its pearlescent color veined with thin lines of electric blue.

"Smell it," he said.

I inhaled. It had a complex, nuanced scent. I sniffed it until it made me sneeze. I thought of luxurious perfumes with layers of scents, distinct notes. But those aromas tend to be experienced successively while the spirit of this flower was, in a manner of speaking, simultaneous: vanilla and dust, moss, sand and musk, the wet interior of a cave, salt and blood.

"It smells like ..."

"Say it."

"It doesn't make sense." I passed the flower to Claudia, and she breathed in. In her expression of amazement, I found what I wanted to say. "It smells like *time.*"

Ekar smiled with his eyes. It was just the answer he had hoped for.

The other guests interrupted us to say hello and buy us a beer. They were cheerful, but not on mushrooms. Some were dancing, others were juggling torches, a few others were playing I don't know what. The smell of the kerosene and smoke made Claudia worry for my lungs. She suggested that we move away from there, but in a bit, Toribio came out and told them to put out the fire. Didn't they realize we were in the middle of the forest?

Ekar told us that on the first day they went out early to collect mushrooms. Toribio showed him the perfect place to find them: out where the cows graze, leaving abundant excrement behind them.

"It's real poetic that cow poop opens portals to consciousness," Ekar admitted, doing a kind of imaginary bow to one of the cows.

Once the friendly ruminants let him take the mushrooms, he shared them with Toribio. He decided not to stay still in the half hour that it took to take effect and walked following the course of the river, watched over by those who, by now, were his friends. At some point he heard someone calling him and advanced to the left side of the forest, confident in the direction he should take. The voice was calling for who he was, he told us.

"But it wasn't calling 'Ekar.' Obviously, it was calling to *me*. The presence, the temporal group of things, of flesh and ideas that I am, I guess. There are a lot of things I don't know how to explain."

The voice speaking to him was a tree.

"I don't know what it's called, or its taxonomy; you can tell us that," he said to me. "But I do know who it is. I recognized it among all the trees, just like I'd recognize you guys in the crowd at the Pino Suárez metro station."

"What did it say?" urged Claudia.

"It said hello," he laughed to himself at how absurd it sounded. "We talked for a bit about a bunch of things that I don't remember anymore. What I do remember is that I started thinking about you." He looked at me. "And then you showed me the flower."

"Me?"

He nodded.

"Like you were there next to me, like I could reach out and touch you."

I watched the sunrise alone, bundled up in the sweater Epifanía had given me the night before. It was windy. The clouds rolled like waves in a real sea. My two friends slept facing me, the rosy pink light illuminating them.

While Claudia and I ate a breakfast of rice atole, Ekar had already stored the modest dose of psilocybin we would be taking in his backpack. In the pockets of my raincoat, I carried my inhaler and the cellphone I had been forced to bring in case of emergency (a familiar euphemism for "in case you get sick"). It wasn't even turned on. It was pointless because Ekar and Claudia didn't have one. On top of that, there was no way I'd get a signal out there.

***

We continued on the path driven by our friend: the path down, the river, the cows. They seemed good enough company to start the trip, so we settled where the left slope of the forest began. Ekar opened his backpack, took out the leaf that held the *water children*. We were cheerful, but ceremonious, trying to show respect for the occasion in a way that would make Epifanía and Toribio proud.

Two men came out from behind the trees. We didn't notice them, despite the fact that we were city girls, constantly on high alert; and Ekar, someone accustomed to surveillance, to being distrusted by the authorities, who always wanted to plant a joint on him so they could blame him for whatever.

The pigs. Cops. They both had tinted glasses and pistols in their belts, which they drummed with their ring-covered fingers.

"What's going on here, son? You're putting your little girlfriends in danger. Bring that shit here. For your own good."

He took the leaf bundle and tucked it between his back and his waistband.

It made me sick that they talked to us like drunk, sketchy uncles, shamelessly giving paternal advice. Claudia stared at them, determined. If she had been standing, she would have towered over them.

"This activity is legal here, following usos y costumbres."

The pigs laughed. Behind them I saw the cows take notice.

"Maybe in your hotel room, mamacita. Here, it's another story. Stand up, sweetheart. Let's see what you've got."

Ekar, who was already standing, handed over his backpack.

"This is all we have. Can I talk with the two of you alone? This isn't their fault."

They rummaged through the bag. They scoffed at the amount of money we were carrying, took what few things we had, and tossed the bags, like thieves, behind them. To the cows.

"Oh, this is all? This is prison, you fucking stoner. Where's the weed? Come on, help your friend out. Which part of his body did he hide it in?"

One of the men pulled Claudia by the arm, and it filled me with rage. I stood in front of them, trembling. The cows were looking at us, and for some reason, that gave me courage.

"Here. This is expensive medication. And this cell phone, too," I said, handing them both objects.

It was a childish, pathetic bargain, but the pigs' eyes brightened. One of the cows, her fur almost red, slowly approached. I looked at Ekar and realized he could see her in my eyes. The men had their backs to her. Ekar did, too, but I could tell that he knew. The cow charged. Ekar took my hand and Claudia's to pull us in the opposite direction from the animal.

One of the cops screamed. They barely had time to move to avoid being rammed. This was not a comedic scene. The man who had grabbed Claudia tried to take out his pistol, but he thought better of it when the animal prevailed and lowered her forehead to attack. They were both scared of this docile beast turned furious protector, or maybe the cops just realized they could run into trouble with the owner of the cattle. Whatever it was, they backed off. As they left, intimidated by the 700-kilo creature that was still coming at them, they kept threatening us.

"If this shit doesn't work, we're coming after you, brat."

"Take it, get high off your asses, fucking bastard kids."

The man threw the leaf bundle to the ground.

The cow didn't take her eyes off of them until they disappeared. Then she returned to grazing right there and after a while went back with the rest. We hugged each other and cried. Then we laughed a lot. The feeling that Ekar knew what was going to happen didn't leave me. I told him.

"I just knew we would be okay. But I should have taken better care of you two," he said, confirming my suspicion.

"What are we going to do without your medicine?" Claudia was more worried about this than I was.

I untied the bundle. The mushrooms were still there, all lined up, innocent.

"We can't do this without a guide," I said. "That should be the lesson." I put them directly into my backpack. Then Claudia pointed out something in the forest.

"Are those the flowers?"

"Yes. That's the tree. There are a lot more than the last time," Ekar answered.

"Let's go look," I said, hoping to boost morale.

The vibrant wild flowers were low to the ground. The scent came in short waves like the earth was exhaling. The play of light on them made them almost iridescent, a color I had never seen on a flower, interrupted suddenly by the electric blue that, I guessed, was the same psilocybin as the mushrooms. Ekar looked up and greeted the tree, its branches full of crosses.

"*Abies religiosa*," I said. "It's a centennial oyamel. A beautiful specimen." We paid the tree our respects. Its crown was lost in the sky.

"We didn't eat any mushrooms, but the flowers still look like they're dancing," Claudia observed.

"How did you take the flower, Ekar? Did you do any research on it?"

"I ate it. Nobody knows. I've asked everyone, and they say that what I felt must have been because of the mushrooms. There are no shamans for this, that I'm sure of."

"But what did you feel? I still don't understand," asked Claudia.

I kneeled on the grass and leaned in to observe them up close. Inflorescences of three, serrate leaves. They were beautiful, strange, and yes, they seemed to dance. I reached to cut one and *poof!* The bud of a nearby flower burst with a strange noise. Its seeds scattered toward me. Because of my surprise and laughter, I got some of them in my open mouth.

"What was that?" Ekar asked.

"I think your flowery friend confused me for a bee. It's like a touch-me-not! It wants me to take its seeds somewhere else," I said, laughing euphorically, full of that layered scent.

"You have blue dots on your face!" Claudia was laughing, too. "It's like blue pollen. It really smells."

"And tastes." An acidic flavor filled my mouth. I started to salivate. I stood up and right away I felt dizzy, nauseous. I looked up to the oyamel, which seemed to rise into infinity, and I noticed it was talking to me, *to my presence, to the group of things, of flesh and ideas that I temporally am.* I knew how old it was, how much it knew about movement; this tree, which to my human eyes appeared static.

One part of me realized what was happening. This same part perceived the stares of Ekar and Claudia, somewhere between fascinated and worried.

"You don't need to eat the flowers. Touch the buds. You just have to receive the seed."

I lay down on the grass and talked to the tree. His language was slow and hushed. Like mine, it depended on air, on breath. He led me to understand many things about patience and perspective, about the multiplicity of lives within mine, him and his ants; me and my bacteria. I wanted to put down roots with my hands, and I noticed what was happening to my skin: it was capable of feeling the slightest pressure, heat, touch. Every blade of grass and every crumb of earth. I heard Ekar and Claudia's voices. They had lain down next to me. I detached my fingers from the ground and searched for one's hand, then the other's. I felt their fingers, I knew them, and my heart skipped a beat. Here were my friends, alive. Nothing had happened to us. I held their hands tight and brought them to my chest. I realized that the most sophisticated evolutionary function of hands was not to manipulate a tool, but to intertwine them with others.

"Thank you for keeping your heart awake," Ekar said to me.

I turned my head to look at his face, and in this movement I could see the faces that the forest hides in all its spiderwebs, all its music. When I finally arrived at his eyes, I heard the nearby spring. I could swear that I heard creatures singing beneath the water, and my heart awoke even more because we were understanding this together. In the hollow of his other hand, my cheek fit precisely, not because of a matter of dimensions, but because it was the moment in time, the precise instant for this hand-shape occupying this space to meet this other cheek-shape, neighbor in this journey, this hour.

I decided to let go of that perfect synchrony, the synchrony of touch, because I understood its nature and extension (the ephemeral eternity, the infinitude within a second), and my body ached for it. But that which I am thanked it, kissing the knuckles of my friend; and I turned, curious, to continue with the discoveries, to taste the air that so many times had denied me oxygen. It smelled of honey, of flowers, of hair and musk, of magnificent dung and grass.

I stuck out the tip of my tongue and kissed its strange inhabitants. I asked them not to abandon me, but the oxygen said it could not make that promise. My back felt the heat of the earth, the millimetric movement of the plates. It warmed my legs, my belly, my head. My hands tried to sink into the rock like they were molten lava. I knew it was possible, but it would take so long that, to achieve it, I would disintegrate into the humus with the worms.

I stood abruptly because I felt the desire not to die, not to disappear, and I had compassion for myself when I realized that this was what I was looking for in my asymmetrical romances, in sex, and I let a bit of my fear vanish. I felt the generous hand of Claudia reach for mine. I heard her before she spoke.

"Are you okay?"

My face turned to answer her, and I found the worms, hard at work, admirable; the birds up there, talking among themselves from the treetops; the tree, congratulating himself on our friendly triangle.

"I'm okay," and my eyes found hers, and I found that she and I were two puppies in the same litter; we tossed each other's hair, bit each other's paws, determined our voluntary kinship in dog language. Ekar's laughter, when he realized we were dogs, was that of a child, and the time of one of us was the time of all three. We were children and we laughed loudly and we always would. Even if we were lost in the woods, the only thing we had to do was intertwine our hands. I gave a giant rock, or rather, he asked me to give him a dance. I don't know how long I floated in the air before falling, but Ekar held me and we spun around and around.

"We danced with the rock to his rhythm!" I said, and when we fell next to Claudia, we three understood a bit more about geological time.

In our mouths we were visited by the tastes of rust and metal and clay and sulfur. Then came other temporal sensations, as if it were a new sense that we were able to experience in who knows what part of us. It wasn't like an event explicitly appeared before our eyes. There were no scenes, nothing like that. It was an intuition to which we attributed an event to come. But the most important revelation was that we could share it if we touched each other, that with our hands intertwined we could decipher together these bitter draughts, or sweet ones, or sour ones. It was a conversation sustained with the senses. We were certain that we would find the meaning through conversing, but with our whole bodies: the radio telescope of skin and hormones and bones.

We fell asleep in the middle of the forest with our hands connected. We had the same dreams, but we woke up every now and then because the effects of the flower came and went like a heavy tide. The strongest wave came at midnight. The white light of the stars split into seven colors and there was a humming in the background. We noticed that between one star and another were extremely fine connections, the threads of a spiderweb made of light and material and gas and time. Little by little, the connections revealed themselves to us, the weaving of events past and future, and we realized that the brightest threads were merely the potential of the future, possibilities that could change. There was no condemnation, no sentence: only probability, mutable and multiple. What bliss.

However, the majority of those visions and intuitions were terrible. It was a startling spectacle to learn that, in reality, *everything was connected*, it was an immense gift: it meant embracing the fullness of compassion.

We understood that skin separated us like the lines of a drawing separates the characters in the background of a comic book. But through it permeates warmth, the essence of things.

"Even the pigs are part of it," we thought together, while we intertwined our fingers with infinite sorrow because the cruel would never touch the peace and wonder that a cow embodies. Everything, at the end of the day, was woven: violence, pain, injustice. Because behind them shine, like a supernova, courage, friendship, and laughter. It all contributed to the perpetual movement and the birth of these flowers. Even our own deaths, but we would understand this better in time.

***

It took us a while to head back because I insisted on botanizing a few specimens of the flower. We returned ecstatic, starving. Toribio and Epifanía invited us to eat with them: tlayudas with beans, tasajo, and quesillo. We told them, incredulous that it all happened that same day, of the encounter with the cops and the mechanism by which the flowers operated, on the exacerbated sensitivity of every feeling, and the matter of time. They didn't understand us very well, but we weren't very clear on it ourselves.

"There must be someone who knows," Claudia and I insisted.

"The only thing I've heard about flowers, since I was a girl, is that it's wise not to play with them: not with the devil's trumpet, or the angel's trumpet, or any of them."

"In any case, we need a guide."

"What if you all have to be the guides now?" Epifanía said. "By the way, I just remembered ..." She left the kitchen and returned with a pillowcase with the words *Providence Keep You* on the borders, surrounded by little flowers just like ours, the threads of colors trying to emulate their iridescent play. She gave it to us.

The next day we felt only a touch of the hypersensitivity that the flower had given us. We left for the beach in Ekar's dilapidated car after effusively saying goodbye to Epifanía and Toribio.

"We'll see each other a lot more," I assured Epifanía. "A little flower told me."

But *providence* was not finished with us. We had to stop several times along the way as new waves came. We didn't know how to measure time while the wave passed through our bodies, left us astonished at the fact of living, at being able to tune into the many melodies of existence.

On the journey we listened to *OK Computer* and *Vespertine*, distraught and joyful. When we felt more like the people we were before, with those names we called each other before all this, we played *Rock en tu idioma Vol. I* and *II* and relaxed.

The sea scared us. It was a sensorial exuberance that turned into absence, like death. Its voice was beautiful, and the pressure that the water exerted on skin was as pleasant as the damp warmth of a body making space for another after longing. We lay in the sand with our hands intertwined to integrate the messages of the sky and the sea. First we witnessed the probabilities of the three of us; then our thread extended until it formed part of the possibilities for humanity as a whole.

"Don't look," Ekar said suddenly, as if we were watching a horror movie. With his other hand he caressed my head and put it on his chest. But the understanding of what was happening was not in sight, but in our union, in our touch. So it was inevitable that I sensed the overwhelming probability that I would die long before they did. Claudia hugged me. It was I who had to console them because I already knew this before the flower.

It took strength to bear witness to the very probable agony of the earth, sickness, the spiritual and physical pain of millions of people, fires, the departure of so many animals, the greenness of the world. But the wave of providence passed on. We walked on the beach, and like a kind of comfort, we watched a few sea turtles, coming and going from the sea, laying their eggs beside us.

We were immature and absent of guides, but we received the seeds. The flower used me as a bee. It was up to me to scatter its seeds so they would sprout elsewhere. When we returned, the waves came farther and farther apart, until we were able to land in our normal lives and even forget a little before the next tide came for us, always preceded by the smell of time. Instead of doing my thesis, I investigated whether providence appeared in any historical archive, but there was nothing about the species anywhere. It felt strange (and tragic) that the knowledge of it was lost or had been destroyed. It had to be somewhere.

I made it the center of my research. I got a new committee, switched advisors. Nobody was too opposed because, seemingly, this was a species never before documented: a flower of the family *Balsaminaceae*, genus *Impatiens*, as I had suspected (though I was mistaken about the psilocybin, it was another substance that I had to research further). I wished it were true. I felt happy and confident about the remnants of our experience, and I told the story to my new advisor with no omissions. I was lucky that she was receptive, though she made a blunt suggestion.

"If you want to keep studying this, you have to be discreet. Just describe it. Keep your methods simple. Be very precise with how you talk about the psychoactive elements: 'it produces this and that effect, observable and quantifiable in this and that way ...'"

"And I could do that with the perception of time?"

She looked at me with a face of pity.

"My advice is that you don't try to explain how it affects consciousness, nothing that doesn't sound like natural science. If you do, they won't let you continue. Believe me. You want some more advice? Don't do this alone. Look for people who are already observing what you want to understand."

It wasn't long before I realized how right she was. When I spoke on the subject, I was always asked why I called the plants "entheogens" and not "hallucinogens" or "narcotics." I explained the etymology created by Wasson and others in 1979 that recognized its ritual use (*entheos*, "god within"), but I was interrupted with a "You don't have to worry about that."

The journey would be long, although, somewhat capriciously, we were able to register it as *Impatiens Synchronica*, not because of the temporal perception that I wanted to emphasize, but under the pretext of its flowering cycle, bound to the reproduction of a certain beetle. In the body, providence also had an annual cycle. That other consciousness bloomed in us each year.

I got my degree, only to confirm that I knew nothing. I was fascinated by the thought that entheogens functioned as chemical keys: they fire up processes in our perception more latent than extraordinary, and the brain even searches for these substances in the organism itself as if they were essential. This idea, which had captivated so many people before me, was silenced by legal prohibitions, not only because of its transforming and destabilizing potential, but because there were those who used this knowledge to create anesthetic empires of business and death, provoking the complete opposite effect. It seems like our bodies are designed to live this experience. We just have to set it in motion. Through the master plants (providence included) nature constantly renews its promise: anyone can have *god within*. There must have been some evolutionary advantage to consuming them. No wonder so many cultures had used them in rituals for centuries.

I asked Epifanía for her help in meeting spiritual masters who could orient me and went to meet with some of these people. Ekar, Claudia, and I also visited places which psychoactive tourism had already transformed into sad markets of spirituality. Their main streets were filled with ads that offered a shamanic version of self-help through mushrooms, ayahuasca, peyote. It was obvious, but we learned it then: to get to the wise people you had to know the people well, let them get to know you, and in some way, deserve the gift to your consciousness, just as it was before those illuminations were excised from their contexts. I discovered nothing that hadn't already been said. Pre-Hispanic cultures developed true technologies of the consciousness, perfecting the tool through attentive observation, experimentation, testing, and the transmission of their knowledge. There was a valuable science there with no *quantifiable* outcomes. A lot of effort went into destroying the world that this wisdom was made for: it was almost extinct.

And seemingly, nobody knew about *Impatiens Synchronica*. It was as if it had sprouted in this century from nothing. I brought it to several masters. Some agreed to try it to help me create a type of guide, a road map that could show other people how it's done. But curiously, it didn't differ much from existing rituals made for other substances, and they overlooked elements that to me seemed fundamental: navigation through time and communion through touch. When I asked what they recommended to experience this to its fullest, one of them shrugged her shoulders and said:

"I don't know. Maybe this flower is from your time, not mine."

Time passed. Claudia, always sensible, set about building a house and a tranquil life to welcome dogs, cats, and beloved people. Ekar became a lawyer (and a Buddhist), got married, and had kids. Even then, the three of us made gaps in productivity, traffic jams, and floods of the city to meet in the tides of providence, to take each other's hands, understand together what we knew would happen and find, in the faintest of probabilities, ways to move forward. We finished our rituals laughing. We called it "shamanistic friendship."

Despite my bad health hindering my trips to the country, I kept investigating the chemical composition of the flower, its cycles and effects, when and where the buds emerged, disobedient (or obedient to a change in climate) on all latitudes like an urgent biological telegram. It was evident that the world was going to hell, and we proved it in the biology and earth sciences departments, eternally ignored Cassandras, but parallel to the academic discussions, an underground interdisciplinary group was forged around the environmental emergency and entheogens. There were people in Medicine, Psychology, Chemistry, Anthropology, and Physics exchanging information and experiences. They didn't know about the *Impatiens Synchronica*. I shared my knowledge of it which, in scientific terms, was nothing. It was time without equations, chemistry without formulas, consciousness without studies of brain waves. To my surprise, they received it with curiosity and gratitude. They were as tired as I was of scientific limitations, and they offered approximations, data, and hypotheses that opened up possibilities.

"It isn't nature's fault it's immeasurable. It's the fault of our need to limit it to what we can measure," concluded a researcher whose work in nanoneurology had been rejected, in which she speculated on the quantum possibility that psychedelics (which is what the radical materialists in the group prefer to call them) were molecular machines capable of boosting the synapses to light speed. This would allow the perception of time, matter, the universe itself on all levels of complexity. The theories would make anyone else nervous, but not us. Vegetalistas, rabbis, shamans, theologists, artists joined the group. We set about criticizing everything New Age, although we accepted the contradiction of our meeting.

I was eager for the next wave of providence to share all of this with Ekar and Claudia, but the gradual combination of deforestation, fierce rains, air pollution, and increasingly aggressive mutations of seasonal virus strains abruptly confined the population, especially defective biologists like me. Life outside and human contact turned lethal. Restrictions to mobility became increasingly severe. After resolving the most urgent necessities of provisions and public health, the new problems we would have to face made themselves known: natural devastation, the accelerated loss of food sources, mental disorders caused by isolation, and the decrease in the global population. The four horsemen of our own apocalypse.

Though I knew that my predicted death was approaching, that it was just a matter of time, fear overcame me. To make things worse, I would experience the final wave of the flower alone. I felt I had failed as a scientist (I couldn't make them listen to the warnings, I couldn't use the knowledge I got from a flower to save the world), as a human (a predatory species that praises beauty while destroying it), as a person (I dedicated my life to trying to understand, but the solitude was too much, and I never felt the peace I had always longed for).

The phone rang. I knew it was Ekar before I even looked at the screen.

"It's time! Have you felt it yet?"

His voice set off the molecular machine, the annual flowering of providence, but we still couldn't smell anything. Waiting for the scent, we talked a bit about the fear and anguish I felt.

"Help me understand," I asked, choking on my words.

"There's no way we can be alone if we're all one and the same. We're separated for a little while by our skin, and nothing more. That's what the flower told us, the tree, the cow, the stars. I mean, that's what we told *each other*, remember?"

And I remembered, and it seemed very clear what that implied: two particles, as far away in time and space as they are, can affect each other simultaneously, synchronously. And if everything is connected, can't we reach for each other, affect each other, touch each other? Be certain, even in the face of our own death, that solitude is impossible?

The scent appeared as an answer.

"I'm going to get Claudia on the call, are you ready?"

***

We were three forms of existence encapsulated in a radio telescope of skin, hormones, and bones. I searched in the ephemeral eternity, in the infinitude within a second, that moment in time, the precise instant when the hand-shapes that occupied their spaces met this other hand-shape. Claudia's voice intertwined her fingers with mine and with Ekar's and together, laughing out loud in the forest of the world, we understood the constrained hope, the evolutionary advantage, the providential miracle of this synchrony of touch.

Conspiracy of the Elements

The rain arrived as long-expected. Not the usual rain that grew the corn, the grass, and the squash. Not the rain that brought golden glimmers in the air at dawn, that invoked the seven colors of the rainbow at dusk. Not the evening storms that, after a while, ran away, thundering and grumbling.

The most dreaded rain arrived, fierce and unstoppable, a scientific prophecy that would flood everything, cause landslides, make people and animals shiver with cold. It would inundate cities all over the world and reduce them to subaquatic ruins, to memories. It rained almost constantly, even when the sun was shining at its highest point in the sky.

But Ayutla was prepared for the anomaly.

The town of Ayutla had spent too much time without running water not to enjoy, at least a little, the possibility of getting soaked, although they knew the situation wasn't a joke, and that there would be danger if they didn't plan to confront all that was coming. They continued dividing up the work they agreed to in their meetings, where the women spoke loud and clear and the rest followed because they knew that the women observed and listened closely to the needs of the community. They were assured that the people, animals, and crops would have sufficient water. In the meantime, they navigated the downpours, contained the landslides, and protected their homes.

They had to adapt, to devise new strategies. They studied the sciences, calendars, and technology they had been developing for ages and took advantage of what they could. When someone shared a new idea or one they had learned somewhere else, they weighed the benefits of implementing it and putting it to the test, such as the lightning rods connected to underground containers, which were still in their experimental stages. Some turned out to be very useful, such as systems for micro-harvesting rainwater into crop strips, which they used to work the land little by little, or extracting water from the air using fog nets (which more than one visitor mistook for volleyball nets).

Others anticipated the worst: what would they do if their houses were flooded, if the hills were washed away? They perfected the art of hydroseeding with mixes of cactus and compost, which hardened the surface but allowed water to filter through and unlike chemicals, wouldn't damage underground water sources. They enticed future plants and future strong-rooted trees to help keep the soil in place and prevent landslides. With patience and effort they became allies with nature's new energy, which had changed in rhythm and mood.

But Ayutla also faced a more complex problem: the constant threat from armed groups who had sequestered their natural springs with the brash tactics of the weak and cowardly, people capable of holding other humans prisoner, who think it's possible to command the forest or slow the momentum of a fire. Apparently, water was not enough for them: they wanted land. To get it, they intimidated the Ayutla comuneras, the owners of the areas most useful to the interests of shady drug and mineral dealers.

The topiles knew how to stand up to them and were vigilant, though they knew that as long as their new, experimental self-defense technologies were still imperfect, they wouldn't be fully protected.

No one knew the lengths people would go to when they stopped listening to the voice of the mountain. It wasn't easy, but the townspeople knew how to organize themselves and keep the peace around them using the harmonious tactics of the strong and brave. The people of Ayutla were not alone: first, because they had themselves; then later, because outsiders learned what they were facing. For years, many had been joining their call, and the name of Ayutla and the water together, fused in the search for justice, were said many times in Ayuuk and in languages that were not Ayuuk.

The threats from armed groups continued despite the new, ceaseless rain until Ayutla began to notice something extraordinary: the town was not suffering the ravages of the weather in the same way their aggressors did. In fact, the jamás conquistados of Ayutla were fine. They had more water, they controlled the technology to use the water and treat it, they had enough food, and their means of containment against the disaster were working: nobody had lost their health, home, or animals, and the streets had not turned to impassable rivers.

Meanwhile, they heard that the armed groups were suffering one accident after another: their guns shot crookedly or went off on their own, injuring their owners. Already deteriorated, the unprecedented humidity the guns were exposed to rusted them and damaged both the mechanism and the ammunition. They couldn't trust, as they had before, those destructive objects in which they once placed their faith and power. In the streets, animals they passed began to jump at them. Without their guns in hand, they couldn't harm or kill them nearly as easily. More subtle vengeance came in the form of piles of badger, tapir, and boar shit hidden in puddles that didn't just make them slip and fall. The falls came with a broken arm or leg. Not to mention the poppy fields: the poor flowers didn't want to push the ground above them to sprout and give them pleasure. They seemed to have, like corrupted cities, like the majority of the "civilized" world, nature furiously pitted against them. And fury they returned, without being fully conscious of the fact that they were only causing more harm to themselves.

One cloudless night, when only a light drizzle fell, a large armed group improvised an attack on Ayutla, unorganized, armed, and fierce.

The leaders of the assembly, the comuneras and the topiles, knew that this was the moment to use everything they had experimented on, thought about, and learned. They got out the self-defense cattle prods they were storing in the underground container of the lightning rod. On contact with those violent but clumsy, erratic bodies that intended to shoot them, the prods released immobilizing electric shocks that twisted their expressions, their hands, into grotesque forms (the older women couldn't help laughing, remembering the macho men who used to act brave by shocking themselves with a machine in the canteen). They disarmed and contained the men. Later, they carried the guns on foot to a rock wall on the edge of their perilous outskirts, a wall the assembly had been well-aware of for a long time, which appeared as unstable and ready to collapse as a house of cards.

The sun rose, and the entirety of Ayutla went to see how it all ended. They decided to perform the final test, the riskiest. The group of women elected for such tasks activated the mechanism of the lightning rod's base that would focus the rest of the accumulated electricity on a specific point, one chosen with intelligence and care.

Everyone's hair stood on end, not only because of the current, but also due to the excitement of seeing how the earth began to tremble lightly under their feet and how the rocks began to fall over the guns, entombing them, as the band played festive chords and people began to dance in celebration, as they hadn't for a long time. Because this long and amiable agreement with the voice of the mountains, with the water and animals and forest, had worked, and their reward was this successful conspiracy of the elements.

THE VISIT

"Are you ready?" I ask myself, feeling strange to be, at last, truly alone with myself. Because that's the exercise, the most important lesson: I have to trust myself. Make the voices that have consoled and advised me, that I've depended on my entire life, merge with my own voice. Now I bring the cup of tea to my lips. I feel the smooth, polished rim molded by the hands of my hosts. I smell the comforting scent of lemon tea, and beneath it, I sense the indecipherable, pulsing notes of another fruit. Maybe it's the secret ingredient that will make The Visit possible.

I'm scared, of course. I'm far from home, from everyone I know. But that's how it has to be. Isolating yourself, sometimes, is the only way to hear your own voice. "So, you're going for who knows how long to the house of who knows who, to be given who knows what to drink, because they'll supposedly *cure your soul*?"

Even the people I thought most understanding surprised me with their judgment. My decision didn't look to them how it did to me: not taking a pause in life, a kind of spiritual retreat, but rather a madness, an imprudent whim. Didn't I realize how risky it was? Taking a long bus ride, then taking local transit, then getting someone in the community to guide me through the dirt paths leading to the almost secret place where a group of older, retired women decided to hide themselves and found a new community, another way to live and organize themselves. Was it really worth it? Some people from the nearby towns called them Nuns; others, Happy Widows; and, of course, there were plenty who called them Witches. Whatever they were, I trusted from the start in the brave experiment they had undertaken that allowed them to be free and even (they said) to help people who needed it.

What does help mean? On the one hand, it's a simple act of feeding. Thanks to the fact that the community shares generous land worked by the strongest women, they have a sufficient and varied agricultural production. Once a week they travel on a joyful excursion to the tracks of the northbound train loaded with migrants that cling to the cars like grapes to a vine. A small committee loads the only truck in the community with baskets full of fruit, bread, casseroles, flavored waters. The women play music at full volume and head out, joking around on the way, to share and feed the *People from the train that the People despise*. I'm repeating the expression that they use because it emphasizes the absurdity of hatred and abandonment between people.

The second way they say that they help is through The Visit, a much more mysterious act, the object of all the suspicion from the outside world.

The Visit is the reason I'm here in the dark with a cup of tea in my hands.

When someone arrives in the community, they open the door, serve them food. Then they ask why the person traveled there. You have to give honest and true reasons, explain what you need and desire. Then they (a group of five or six) just listen. If, after consulting among themselves, it seems proper, one of the women takes the person into her home. The next day the person will sleep and live as a guest in another home. And so, an indefinite number of days after going back and forth, participating in the daily work of the field, the care of the animals and the house and the preparations to feed the Train People, the hosts return to the table to address the matter. Then they speak sincerely. They tell the person what they've seen in her, in her mood, in her conduct, in her way of being and doing. It's not always nice, of course. Only then do they tell her whether they have decided to gift her with the experience of The Visit or not.

So far, the "nuns" or the "happy widows" or the "witches," that is, the women of this community, have rejected as many people as they have accepted.

Many people who have done The Visit don't return to their previous life.

Only two out of some fifty over the course of fifteen years have been men.

What accounts for this difference? Well, the women are very discreet with respect to what they observe in those they consult. But many speculate that it has to do with seeing the good disposition to complete the work necessary to sustain the community and to help the Train People. I wouldn't be so sure of this. Some of those who arrived to ask for help couldn't even get out of bed during their stays. But if they make anything clear, it's that seemingly, we need more solitude, more silence.

More repair.

Because The Visit is a method *to cure the soul* (I'm using their words again), people on the outside, therapists or researchers, describe it as a type of self-healing of the psyche. They compare The Visit with treatments that allow people to return to the traumatic episodes of their lives using regressive hypnosis, so they can defend or console themselves in key moments, diminishing the effects of trauma in the present. What is controversial, and the reason it's stigmatized as, at the very least, irresponsible (and it seems to me, disproportionately, like a dangerous cult) is that the experience is too vivid, too intense. Some have described it as a trip through time and space achieved through a combination of factors: the strategic positioning of a room within certain geographic coordinates, the consumption of a special drink, and the timely intervention of an unknown technology, a certain ancestral artifact that is impossible to see, only to manipulate, maybe made of stone and quartz, that produces a whitish flash of light when the arrangement of its pieces is adjusted.

The people who support this theory are convinced that they were there: they could smell, touch, breathe, and above all, talk to themselves (breaking the convention of time travel that is normally portrayed in fiction).

Despite all this, The Visit is not carried out under the supervision of any mental health specialist or through the guidance of a witch doctor, to mention a less orthodox therapeutic tradition. The women of the community don't intervene more than to decide if a person can complete it or not. In the case of the former, they are in charge of preparing The Visit, of being, so to speak, only the hosts, the custodians of a transcendental experience.

I've already passed the first interview, where I didn't have to tell them the five episodes of my life where I would like to make The Visit. It wasn't necessary. They make you feel like they know the kinds of things that have happened to you. I spent the nights in different houses, the hard work of caring for the land; the work, unexpectedly moving for me, of feeding the turkeys, of taking the sheep out to walk in the fog and dew. I cut the corn and the tomatoes for food; I learned to pack, first clumsily, then efficiently and proudly, the tamales and the fruit that we tossed to those who couldn't get off of the moving train. I shared, because I couldn't do anything else, their hungry stares, their pained feet, their uncertainty. Their pain. I mopped (badly) the floors of houses that were not mine and heard the burden of age, of solitude, but also the liberty and the serenity of these women. One night we got drunk, danced, and even composed "colorful" rhymes. Some of us doubled over in laughter.

When I sat with them in the common kitchen to find out whether they would invite me to make The Visit, I knew that, in their eyes, I deserved it, not for having worked hard or for being a good person, far from it, but because I needed it, because my soul was willing to learn, to listen. That, I would say, is the requirement, but I'm sure it's different for each person. I know these women know what they're doing because they've lived well. That is to say, they've done well, but also made mistakes. They've asked for forgiveness and also forgiven. But above all, they've learned to be alone with themselves. They know that the presence of others in our lives is an event with fleeting frequency, sometimes joyful, sometimes violent. They know that the permanence of ourselves within ourselves, however, is inevitable. Perhaps, even eternal. And that when you understand this, when you live it, you can truly accompany others in their journeys.

When I confessed that I was scared of going back and being paralyzed, unable to defend myself, unable to do anything for myself and, therefore, The Visit not working, one of them set me straight. She told me I shouldn't fool myself: it's impossible to change what happened. But it is possible for me to be with myself at any time, anywhere. Sometimes it's the solitude of helplessness that hurts us, that leaves us defenseless. And in the future there will be other times when nobody, nobody but ourselves, can be there for us. Like in the hour of our deaths.

I don't understand those who think there are no guides in The Visit. Doesn't all of that, everything they said, imply being there, showing the way, holding on for the discovery, within yourself, of your own strength?

Today, first thing in the morning, the entire community brought me to where it happens. Only one of them guided me through an underground tunnel into a large, cozy room. The door shut softly behind her, the last person who would see me in who knows how many hours or days. She took the only light from the room, which illuminated her friendly gesture before leaving; a serene smile and a wink to encourage me. I could choose whether to lock the door. They could open it if necessary. Then everything was dark. I thought that after a while, when my eyes adapted, I would see silhouettes of the jar of water and the wash basin, the bed carefully made with sheets steeped in lavender water and dried in the sun, the other door that led to the toilet (nothing is overlooked here).

But I don't see anything. There is no gap for light to come through. The temperature is warm and the air, smelling like fresh clay, is clean and satisfactory. Even the darkness is comfortable.

"Are you ready?" I ask myself. I'm scared, of course, but not because I'm here, far away from all the people I know. I fear reliving it, all the moments in time I chose to Visit. I'm afraid of hearing my own voice. But that's the exercise, the most important lesson: I have to trust myself.

I bring the cup of tea to my lips. With my other hand, I make sure I have within reach the little device that will set everything in motion. It looks so ordinary: a case carved from jade, a jewelry box containing something else, a little Rubik's cube jingling like a rattle filled with pebbles. I drink a sip of lemon tea. Underlying it, I feel the indecipherable notes of fruit pulsing, fruit that I plucked from a bush myself.

Carefully, I set it to one side, take the object and turn the pieces as instructed. I hear a snap within the case, and the snap produces a light that lets me see, for an instant, the figures painstakingly etched on its surface. The room starts to color, to illuminate like an unfocused film, or rather the way dawn and the world come into existence when we open our eyes from sleep.

I'm there, in that place, twice: here, like a ghost, and there, tiny and tangible, four years old, playing in the toy room of a house I know well, a house filled with joy but also fear, pain. The door opens, a head leans in, its silhouette familiar to me. I thought that, when this moment came, I would cry, scream, take the girl, and bring her with me far from here. But none of that happens. We just look at each other. The only thing that matters is to smile at her, stroke her hair. To look myself in the eye and say: "It's okay. I'm here with you."

They Will Dream
in the Garden

Long and short-term goals:

—Get into swimming
—Work hard to pay school enrollment fees
—Scrape up money for El Cervantino
—Build the closet
—Paint the house in September
—Buy dining room chairs
—Buy some shoes
—Read Plato
—Talk to and be friendly with people

Handwritten note by Erika Nohemí Carrillo (in a photograph by Mayra Martell)

The orange trees will be heavy with fruit, and their blossoms will fill the humid air of the western garden. A silky fog will cool the tips of the blades of grass growing in that meadow. The sun will always come out behind the almond tree, and the branches of the oldest tree, a stocky ahuehuete, will extend first toward its rays, stretching like a girl who wants to wake up. Around nine, the garden will fill with silhouettes. Some will greet each other. Others will be frightened by the falling of an orange, and they will run away laughing toward the shadows of other leaves. A few more will look toward the sea that, beneath the slope that elevates the western garden above the beach, will roar and extend far enough to climb the grayish blue sky.

The assistants will check that everything is in good condition to receive the visitors because in the mid-morning many groups of first-graders will arrive accompanied by their teachers, some of them still apprentices. They will come out of the vehicles amid shouts of excitement and stumbling. The apprentice teacher will warn them, "No running!," with a girl in his arms who has fallen asleep during the trip, her mouth half-open and her cheeks flushed.

The Caretaker of the garden, a smiling old woman with a steady gait despite using a walking stick, will give the assistants the usual instructions: support the apprentice teachers at all times, guide the children through their emotions, have the snacks ready at two, every hour distribute water for the children to sip. Later she will quicken her step and stand at the front of a long line of children who will sing thunderously and off-key, a joyful procession, down the pebbled path before arriving at the western garden. Some children will lose the rhythm. One girl will get distracted by a lizard hiding beneath a rock, and the apprentice teacher will have to guide them back to the path, pacing their steps, clapping. The small steps will be heard in unison over the gravel. The children's laughter will float in the air, mixed with the scent of honey and the salty aftertaste of the breeze. The temperature will be very pleasant, a comforting warmth.

At the tall brass gate that guards the garden, the party will stop. A few teachers will continue entertaining the children, the rest turning to listen to the warnings of one of the place's assistants.

"As you all already know, the idea is to let the children interact with them and intervene only when necessary. Do not be afraid of the reactions of the children or try to limit them, they are part of the educational process. We will be close by and aware of their needs at all times."

The brass doors will open slowly with the magnetic key that The Caretaker wears as a necklace. The juvenile commotion will disperse through the western garden until the children notice the presence of *them*.

Their silhouettes will shine with pearly glimmers that will enchant the visitors. They will be made, like all the old tricks are, of lights and mirrors, a complex mechanism that will remain hidden to the visitors. In the open air they will possess a subtle transparency which, at first, will allow a view of the landscape through them, but a closer look will make one appreciate their defined features. They will seem solid, *alive*. Beneath a tree will be the ones who study; others who play will be moving from side to side; those who are speaking to others will be sitting on the grass. If they move too fast, they will emit a tenuous glow, leaving a brief luminous wake in their steps.

The Caretaker will walk toward the apprentice teacher, who will continue juggling the sleeping girl in his arms, and the boy who clings to his leg like an anxious puppy.

"Do you need help? You could share a bit of that love," she will say to him as she opens her arms as if to receive the girl.

"Thank you. Maybe one of the assistants could help me check if I have something on my right leg. Oh, it feels so heavy! What could it be? I think I've been climbed by a Tomasito!"

The boy in question will be so entertained by the joke that he will persist even more with the game. But finally, one of the assistants will take him with her. The Caretaker and the apprentice teacher will lose them among the rest of the people and the silhouettes.

"You're very kind. I'd like to take this opportunity to tell you that it is a true honor to meet you, ma'am. Your work in ..."

The Caretaker of the garden will smack her lips and with a gesture, ask him not to continue because she will find the recognition uncomfortable for reasons other than mere modesty. But since she won't want the man to feel slighted, she will take him by the arm so they can walk together.

Marisela, better known as The Caretaker, was born in September of 1985, in Veracruz. She was the last of three children. Her favorite memory of that time was hanging the laundry out in the sun with her mother: the smell of soap, the sound of the fabric as it unfurls like the wings of a bird, and also the games of her mother, who disguised herself as a ghost hiding under the bedsheets to scare her. This way they forgot about their daily routine, which was tiresome. Every day Marisela and her mother served the meals and ironed her brothers' shirts, who took them to the movies when they had time, on special occasions.

One night in her relatives' house, one of her mother's brothers entered the room where she slept. She didn't know exactly what it was the man was doing, standing there next to her in the dark because she was too little to understand. She got the impression that her uncle was wringing out what he had between his legs like a wet rag. She was scared, but she never told anybody. And she felt guilty for keeping a secret.

When she was fifteen, she and her mother moved to Mexico City by themselves. Marisela had to get a job to support them, first in a shoe store. Her boss soon wanted *something else* from her; he said as much, spitting into her ear between stacks of merchandise in the stockroom, smelling of new leather. She quit. During the truck ride home, she was so worried about what would become of them that she didn't realize, not until much later, that a man had put his hand between her legs.

Thanks to her uncle—the one who had done *that* in her room—she started working at a Big Telecommunications Company. At first it was simple to answer telephones and push buttons, but then technological advances complicated everything. They fired many girls who didn't know how to use the new machines (among them was Paquita, a friend of hers who was also from Veracruz). She decided she would take every class available. At night she studied the functions of cables and computers, of mirrors and laser lights. She wanted to learn the inner workings of what the company called "the image of the future," holograms. She got the highest grades in her classes. She got promoted. Married. She had kids. Her husband was "a good man," if being a good man meant he washed his own underwear and cared for her and her daughters if they were sick, made dinner once in a while, and almost never scolded her for spending too much time outside of the home.

The Caretaker and the apprentice teacher will watch a typical scene: the boy will run, playfully touch the silhouette, and immediately pull his hand away.

"Hey, don't do that, Tomás! You don't even know her, yet. Say hello to her, tell her your name first." The tone of the assistant will not be reproachful and will try to ignore the child's pouting caused by the electric current.

The apprentice teacher will want to approach Tomás, but The Caretaker will hold him back.

"I'm sure this thing about touching wasn't around in your time. The first thing the children tend to do is put their hands through them, but when they cross the field, the system emits a current. The stings aren't very pleasant, but they're tolerable. They always think twice before putting their little hands in again. The instruction at all times is that they treat them just like real people."

"I understand." The apprentice teacher will then furrow his brow, considering a new problem. "But what if they want to hug them?"

The Caretaker will offer him a melancholy smile.

"They can't. It's part of the lesson."

It will be a little hard for the apprentice teacher to understand why. But in the end, he will concede its logic: the dead will never be able to receive our affection again. Not even them, even if they're "back."

One morning Marisela arrived to work and was met with the news that Paquita had been murdered in the State of Mexico. They found her body recently discarded on the sidewalk like people do when a run-over animal gets in the way. They had done horrible, horrible things to her.

Paquita had gripped in her fist the keys to her house, the place where she hoped to return. She had used them to defend herself. What if she was up to no good, they said, what was she doing alone at that hour? But what if she were on her way to work! said Marisela, and if she had been up to "no good" (and it would be your fault, because you fired her, although she didn't say that), so what? She deserved it?

The rest shrugged their shoulders. They quickly returned to their own business. But she still could not stop seeing Paquita's absence nor the corpses of one woman after another and another. There were too many. And all of them, in the eyes of decent people, seemed to be at fault for what had happened to them. They didn't even mention their names in the newspaper articles: "Drug Addict Murders His Mother," "Ex-Girlfriend Slain out of Spite," "Woman Who Reported Rape Killed for Gossiping."

The key will be in combining the dynamics of play and conversation to keep the children's attention. The teachers will show affection to convey safety. And although they will keep their distance, they must be within reach at all times.

"Hello, what's your name?"

"Tomás, but everyone calls me Tomasito. What do people call you?"

"My name is Rubí Marisol, and everyone calls me Rubí. What pretty eyes you have, Tomás."

"My mom packed cookies in my lunch. Want one?"

"I would, but I can't eat."

"Why not?"

"Because I don't have a body like you." She'll join her hands in front of herself with her palms facing upward and then slide one across the other, passing right through. "See? But we can still talk."

The boy will be perplexed. He will try to do the same and then will want to touch Rubí's silhouette, but he'll remember that the sensation is not pleasant.

The apprentice teacher will seem uncomfortable with the situation. The Caretaker will try to alleviate the tension.

"Do you remember the first time you came here?"

"Yes. I've never forgotten it. I was ten. But bringing them at this age seems dangerous. They don't have all the cognitive tools yet to understand the significance of this place. We haven't even told them the meaning of death, let alone the death of all of them."

The Caretaker will listen attentively. Meanwhile, she will observe the numerous tiny white butterflies that fly around the silhouettes, the children, the flowers. They will look beautiful, but she can't stop wondering if they aren't, perhaps, an infestation.

One day they found the body of Dulce, who worked Monday through Friday cleaning offices, including Marisela's office, in order to pay for her computer studies on weekends. Dulce's friends—most of them just girls, not even fifteen—started meeting every Tuesday to remember her and to practice punches, kicks, slaps, whatever kind of defense would protect them.

Those first days they finished the sessions with red faces, disheveled and sweaty, crying together from pure fear or pure courage. After a couple of months, they laughed a bit more, punched harder, and finished their training by eating something sweet to recover. They looked for a name. They liked The Gossips because it was a word people used to judge them, to tell them to conform, that they'd better sit still and shut up. One evening Marisela came to the door and asked to join the group. Those girls taught her to kick hard in her stockings and uniform and everything, to jab with her elbows, to be brave and to cry in good company.

"Why don't you have a body?"

"Because it was taken from me. I'm dead."

When she detects the boy's silence, the silhouette of Rubí will give more concrete answers.

"That means that I can't eat or play or kiss my mom."

The boy will look around, as if searching for some clue. He will look toward the sea, and then he'll study the appearance of the person speaking to him.

"Are you a ghost?"

"No. I'm a memory. Like a photograph."

"Like an old-time video?"

"Yes, exactly that. Tomás, do you have grandparents?"

The boy will ignore the question.

"Why were you killed?"

"I don't know. Why do you think it happened?"

Tomás will think of the answer, pursing his lips, furrowing his eyebrows.

"Because you did something bad. Maybe you made someone really, really mad."

The silhouette of Rubí will consider those options.

"It wasn't my fault. It was they who did something very bad."

"They hurt you?"

"Yes."

"Did your mom make it better?"

"When you're killed, it can't be made better."

The Gossips made a pact: they would take care of each other. Violent boyfriends or fathers, abusive bosses? Let's see if they can take all of us at once. When one of them asked for help, the rest would show up en masse, making it clear to her aggressor that they would not let her fight alone. They grew until they formed an army made of women of all ages who went where their presence was needed. They started to appear in the news, to be taken seriously, to give advice.

The years passed, and Dulce's friends, those high school girls, turned into mature women who made people listen, who demanded justice. People learned to look at them with respect, and that respect was slowly extended to the rest of the women like the moisture of ocean waves reaching the hot distant sand.

Marisela got older, too. She kept working at the Big Telecommunications Company in her laboratory of mirrors and laser lights. She saw her daughters grow up, she saw her mother die, always accompanied by her friends. A longing arose inside her. She had a plan.

The apprentice teacher will also notice the white butterflies, the unpredictable dance of their flight, the scent of flowers and salt that will float through the western garden. He and The Caretaker will enjoy all of it while the assistants have the children sing a very old song, one that will talk of planting a seed and leaving it to grow in peace and knowing to wait to see what it becomes.

"You're probably right," The Caretaker will say, in response to his worry about the age of the children. "And the people who decided to start bringing them at earlier ages were also probably right. Learning that there are different paths in life, that there are alternatives to violence, takes time. Better to start immediately, I guess." She will shrug her shoulders.

"You don't sound so sure ..."

"I am. It's just that, in the beginning, the point of this place was different."

Marisela's plan consisted of gathering resources to construct the holographic memorial she designed along with The Gossips and other organizations who carried a reliable record of the victims. Every one of the murdered women, with her body and her name, would be replicated in a three-dimensional hologram using testimonies and materials provided by their families, friends, and above all, the information recovered from their personal email and social media accounts: photographs, videos, letters, conversations ... everything would be used to recreate as precisely as possible their voices, movements, reactions: to, in some way, *bring them back to life*.

If they got enough money, they could use more advanced technology that would allow them to set up the system outside in nature. Maybe in a garden by the sea. It would have to be a beautiful place, the closest thing to a paradise that they could give to them and their families, to remember them alive and happy.

The apprentice teacher will imagine the placid memorial that this garden once was. He will appreciate the idyllic scenery with its trees and its beach, the peaceful wandering of the silhouettes.

"The place is just as beautiful as I remembered. There are more trees, sure, the ones we planted have grown. Everything is very well preserved."

"It's true," The Caretaker will respond proudly. "Although I don't know what's more astonishing: that its beauty is being preserved or that it's being preserved *in Mexico.*"

The apprentice teacher will laugh, more because of the ease with which she says these things than because of the joke itself. He will not think it implausible that Mexico could keep anything in good condition. Between her generation and that of the apprentice teacher, there will be an abyss.

"It must be surprising for you to see how the country has changed. You've seen it all."

"Well, I'm 94 years old. If I hadn't seen it all, I'd ask for a refund on my entrance fee."

"I imagine those times must have been terrible."

"Yes, they were."

There was a time when nobody called them *silhouettes*. Their families came to visit them and felt almost happy. Marisela saw The Gossips' wish fulfilled when their mothers and fathers, their sisters and brothers, and their friends saw them in the garden, *alive*, smiling. They felt the joy that justice had not been able to give them. As is natural, many families disappeared with the passing of the years, swept away by the river of life, by their work, their loved ones. But some never returned because the garden did not compensate them at all. "It's not them," they said.

The problem was that Marisela had been naïve. It wasn't possible to make up for everything. From some of them, they barely had a name, a blurry photograph. From others, there were only bones. Those who had left an ample testimony of their path through the world made almost perfect, precise holographic replicas, but even then, a life is a unique weave, a thread within a great tapestry, and if it breaks, the thread that replaces it will not be the same. It isn't possible to patch up their flesh, blood, breath, knowledge, desire. Their future.

When few families were left, the State decided that the memorial should serve an additional function to earn the right to permanence. It would serve as an educational space against violence. The younger population would come, by obligation, to learn the history of the murdered women of Mexico with the purpose of it never happening again. The Caretaker understood the reason for this change, and what's more, as one of The Gossips, she would believe it necessary. But she detested the feeling that they were being used. She refused to reprogram them, to turn them into chapters in a textbook. She cried and fought to keep them intact.

In the end she had to do it so their memory wouldn't disappear. From that point on, the silhouettes would have to repeat to the children, time and time again, that they were dead.

"The country moved forward because of people like you, people who never gave up demanding justice."

The Caretaker will make another incredulous gesture.

"There's no merit in that. It was the only thing we had left. So much horror left us with no purpose, no meaning. Conserving the memory was the only way out."

"At least the deaths of all those women were good for something."

Clinging to her cane, The Caretaker will turn brusquely to respond.

"Good for something? For what? To teach us that we're a horror? We already knew that. It's one thing to voluntarily give your life for a cause and another to be killed for it. Which would you like more? That your life had been 'good for something' or to have lived? To bite an apple, to smell the rain on the earth, to see the ocean. I don't know. As I get older, I think transcendence is overrated. It's a comfort of fools, a comfort for the living, but not for the dead. If they could really speak (*them*, not the silhouettes), what would they say to us? 'Listen, it's nice that my death was good for something, but I didn't want to die.' This," she will say, extending her arms and the cane, as if trying to encompass the whole garden, "is not enough. How can I fix the damage? Can you imagine that they used to pile them up in a tower of anonymous bodies? Can you believe that they were blamed for their own deaths? Nobody can imagine the pain they experienced in their final moments, and you all, the young, don't understand the horror of knowing that the men who did it weren't monsters. It wasn't Jack the Ripper. It was their classmates, their boyfriends, their relatives, the friendly taxi driver you chatted with yesterday, the police officer on the corner. It was the world, a society that made us beauty queens while they kicked us in the ribs and called us crazy if we complained. That's how horrible it was."

The apprentice teacher will listen to the reprimand without looking at her face. He will look at the children, who will keep digging holes in the dirt, singing the old sowing song.

"I'm sorry, it's true. Of course, they didn't die in vain." The Caretaker will let out a long sigh before continuing. "The anger when we lost them was the start of it all. We rose up, chanted their names in the streets, we managed to change the course. They were the wind that propelled the sail of this boat, of our future. I just wish that we had learned the lesson sooner, that all of them could have kept living. That they could have had, at least, a chance to do what they dreamed of."

The apprentice teacher will look into her eyes and respectfully agree. He will note that many silhouettes are listening to the singing children and even applauding them; others continue about their business mechanically, somewhat estranged from the present, trapped in the programming of the tasks that they themselves chose a long time in the past, when they were alive and confessed, in the many spheres of online life, what they liked, what they did or what they wanted for the future. He will rummage through his memory.

"You know what I want to do? Study to be an engineer," Mariana Elizabeth had said to him when he was a ten year-old boy (he never forgot her name).

"I don't really know what that is."

"Someone who builds things, like bridges or machines."

"If you study, my mom says that, when you grow up, you can be whatever you want."

"I'm not going to grow up because I'm dead. But how I would like to ..."

The seed song will end. He will ask the children to gather up everything and say goodbye. They will react in various ways. Some will start to cry, some will say goodbye with an indifferent gesture. A few girls will want the silhouettes to keep their drawings.

The apprentice teacher will have to approach Tomás because he will sense his confusion. He will be there, staring at nothing. Before he takes a step, the boy will wrap his arms around the silhouette and feeling nothing, will hug himself inside Rubí's luminous form.

"I want to hug you because it's really mean that they killed you. I want to hug you because they hurt you and left you all alone."

Tomás will feel the electrical currents through his whole body and will resist them until the apprentice teacher takes his hand, separates him from Rubí.

At six in the evening, the sun will begin to set in the western garden. The visitors will have to go just as the darkness arrives, which will make the silhouettes even more beautiful. Their luminous colors will be striking, refined and clear, against the night sky. They and the children will wave goodbye, and for The Caretaker everything will look like a movie from way back when everything was happy and people on the dock waved goodbye to the boat setting sail and there was music and streamers.

The assistants will make sure that everything is clean and in order before leaving. Marisela, who will insist until the end of her days that she be the one who leaves last each day (they call her The Caretaker for a reason), will wander around the garden as she always does, making a sound with her cane on the stone paths, resting every so often against a tree.

With the magnetic key that she wears around her neck, she will lock the brass doors that separate the control room from the garden. The silhouettes will sleep by the sea, lying on their sides, mouths half-open, hands under their chins or on their laps, a pretty illusion that occurred to her when she updated some of the systems, an image that, day by day, allows her to stop the motors without the feeling that she's unplugging them, erasing them, that the world will once again be without them. This way it will be like she's turning off the lights so they can sleep after she tells them a story. Oh, if only life would allow her to finish the program that would allow them to dream! But Marisela, just like The Gossips, is already very old, and there are still so many details to take care of. Others will have to finish it and take the risk of putting it into action. During the day they will be heroines, silhouettes, memories. They will say that they are dead, but the nights will be theirs. They will construct what was taken from them. In the garden they will dream of their future.

Marisela will watch them sleep. And then she will press the button. The silhouettes will shrink until they become miniscule points of light mixed up with the stars that hang over the sea. In a while everything will be dark without them.

"Rest, my girls," The Caretaker will murmur. "Rest."

Acknowledgements

I sincerely thank all the people who took care of me during the writing of these stories, especially my family and friends (cats included). Many of your actions, gestures and words are here as a way of witnessing the love that is in the world. It is perhaps the most valuable part of this book.

To all the people who carefully read these stories and who, with their generosity, significantly improved them, trusted them, translated them and took them to other landscapes, particularly Verónica Murguía, Alberto Chimal and George Henson, who included in Latin American Literature Today Adrian Demopulos's translation of "Soñarán en el jardín". I am very grateful to Adrian, of course, for being the wonderful medium in that arduous and mysterious act that is translation. I'm very grateful to Arrate Hidalgo, Margaret McBride, Ritch Calvin and Marina Berlin for awarding "They Will Dream in the Garden" with the James Tiptree, Jr. Award (Otherwise). Thanks also to all the people who received this story with attention and warmth (and filking!) at Wiscon.

Huge gratitude to Bill Campbell, for trusting me and making this book possible through his patience and hard work. Many thanks to John Picacio and Lauren Raye Snow for such a beautiful cover. Thanks to the entire Mexicanx Initiative for their warm presence and support.

And thanks to you, reader, no more a stranger, the other half of my imagination. This is for you, too.

Gabriela Damián Miravete

ABOUT THE AUTHOR

Mexico City native Gabriela Damián Miravete writes fiction and essays that have been translated to English, Italian, Portuguese, French, and published in *A Larger Reality/ Una realidad más amplia* (part of the Hugo Award Finalist project The Mexicanx Initiative Scrapbook), *Boundaries & Bridges: The Wiscon Chronicles Vol. 12* (Aqueduct Press) and the World Fantasy Award Finalist anthology *Three Messages and a Warning: Contemporary Mexican Short Stories of the Fantastic* (Small Beer Press). She won the Otherwise Award (formerly James Tiptree, Jr. Award) for the short story "They Will Dream in the Garden". She loves working in collaborative projects such as the art & science collective Cúmulo de Tesla and Mexicona: Imaginación y Futuro, a speculative fiction literary festival in Spanish. Gabriela spends (maybe too much) time listening to rocks, whales, and what Fellini and Chewbacca, her two cats, have to say about life on planet Earth.

About the Translator

Adrian Demopulos was born in Dallas, Texas. She has an MFA in Literary Translation from the University of Iowa. Her translations have appeared in *Latin American Literature Today* and in the anthology *A Larger Reality: Speculative Fiction from the Bicultural Margins* by The Mexicanx Initiative. She received a Tiptree Award special honor for translating the 2019 winning story, "They Will Dream in the Garden" by Gabriela Damián Miravete.